THE SECRET OF MOON CASTLE

The boys tiptoed outside into the moonlight, and hurried round the corner to pick up the pillow that had been thrown out of the window. As they did so, Jack looked up at the tower, and got the surprise of his life! There was a light on in the top floor window – which meant that someone must be up there! In the tower, where Mrs O'Moon said no one went because it was dangerous! Who was it? Could it be Fin? Or someone else entirely?

"Come on!" he said to Tom. "There's someone up in the tower! Quick! Let's go up there and find out who it is!"

*Other titles available
in this series:*

Enid Blyton's™

THE SECRET OF MOON CASTLE

4

Screenplay novelisation
by Alex Parsons

Collins
An imprint of HarperCollinsPublishers

For further information on Enid Blyton™ please contact
www.blyton.com

Original screenplay by Harry Duffin

This screenplay novelisation first published in
Great Britain by Collins 1998
Collins is an imprint of HarperCollins*Publishers* Ltd
77-85 Fulham Palace Road, Hammersmith,
London W6 8JB

1 3 5 7 9 8 6 4 2

ISBN 0 00 675318-3

Enid Blyton's signature mark and
Mystery & Adventure are trademarks of
Enid Blyton Ltd.

Printed and bound in Great Britain by
Caledonian International Book Manufacturing Ltd,
Glasgow G64

CHAPTER ONE

The garden at Peephole was alive with the sound of children's laughter and the excited yapping of Prince, the Arnolds' dog. The twins, Laura and Mike, rushed around like demented windmills chased by their elder sister, Peggy. Their best friend Jack, who lived with them because he had no parents of his own, had craftily shinned up a tree to avoid capture.

"Gotcha!" Peggy tagged Mike.

Peggy and Laura sprinted away from him in the blink of an eye. Mike looked round and his gaze fell on Ruby, their nanny, sitting on the garden bench, enjoying the late summer sunshine and resting her bandaged ankle on a stone mushroom. Mike raced over to her and touched her arm.

"You're it, Ruby!" he shouted as he dashed away.

"Oi! That's not fair!" she laughed, but she hobbled to her feet nonetheless and limped after them. The children stood around her in a circle, just out of reach, taunting her to catch them. Ruby lunged at each of them in turn, but it was no use. She collapsed in a heap on the lawn, out of breath.

"Come on, Ruby!" encouraged Mike.

"I'm too old to play 'tag'," she moaned. "I'm thirty, not thirteen."

Laura rushed over and put her arms around Ruby. "Mike, that wasn't fair, picking on Ruby."

"Hey, when I was your age…" began Ruby.

"…you weren't in the habit of falling off your boyfriend's motorbike!" added Mike.

"All right, all right!" grinned Ruby. "Don't rub it in!"

At that moment, the children's father, Thaddeus Arnold, appeared in the doorway waving a sheet of paper.

"Hey, you lot! Anyone interested in my news?"

"I bet he's going away exploring again," muttered Mike.

"What is it, Dad?" shouted Peggy.

"Aha!" said Thaddeus mysteriously, disappearing back into the house with his paper.

"Typical!" snorted Peggy. "He's up to his old tricks again." The children started towards the house.

"Hey! Isn't anyone going to help *me*?" asked Ruby, still sitting on the grass and fighting off

Prince's valiant attempts to lick her to death. Jack and Peggy rushed back to help her up.

"What's it all about, Ruby?" asked Jack.

"I dunno, love, really I don't," she replied.

Thaddeus stood in his kitchen, surveying his unruly brood as they took their places round the kitchen table. He smiled at Ruby, who looked after his children while he went off on his numerous expeditions to strange parts of the world, and tried to look sternly at the children. He cleared his throat importantly.

"Get on with it, Dad!" said Peggy.

"I'm waiting for silence," he replied.

The kids took the hint and sat as quiet as mice. Thaddeus cleared his throat again and read from the piece of paper he'd been clutching so tightly.

> *"Dear Mr Arnold,*
> *I have to inform you that your*
> *application to adopt Jack*
> *Bennett into your family…"*

Thaddeus peered over the top of the paper and paused for effect. The children's eyes were as big as saucers. Jack bit his lip.

"...has been approved."

His last words were drowned by deafening cheers. Jack was delighted, but speechless.

"Jack, Jack, you're my big brother now!" Laura threw her arms around him.

Jack grinned at her and hugged her back. "There's always a drawback!" he smiled. "Now you'll have to do as you're told!"

"Some hope!" said Ruby, joining in the group hugs.

The back door opened and Charlotte Clancy poked her head around the door. "Can anyone join in the fun?" she asked.

"Charlie!" exclaimed Thaddeus, his face lighting up at the sight of her.

"I knocked, but nobody heard," she explained. Laura, who loved Charlie, rushed over to embrace her. Charlie was a photographer and journalist who often worked with her father when he went off exploring. Laura, who was very sensitive to atmospheres and feelings, in people as well as places, had noticed that her father brightened up considerably whenever Charlie was around.

"We've adopted Jack," she explained to Charlie. "He's my big brother now."

"Oh, brilliant!" exclaimed Charlie. "Congratulations, Jack! Or should it be commiserations – joining this madhouse?"

"Exactly!" grinned Jack. "There's no hope for me now!"

Charlie went over to Thaddeus and touched his shoulder. "Well done, Thad," she said softly.

"Welcome to the family, Jack." Thaddeus shook his newly-adopted son's hand.

"Thanks, Dad," said Jack, giving him a hug in return.

"Well," said Charlie, "that rather puts my surprise in the shade."

"What is it, Charlie?" asked Peggy.

Charlie held up a brochure. *Irish Castles* read the title in a suitably Celtic script. Jack took it from her and studied the pictures of romantic towers, castellated battlements and lush green grass.

"The magazine's asked me to do a feature on the castles of Ireland, so I'm going over for a couple of weeks."

"Can we come too?" asked Peggy.

"Well, that's the surprise," smiled Charlie. "How would you lot like a holiday in a real Irish castle?"

"Fabulous!" cried Peggy. "Can we, Dad?"

"Well, I—" began Thaddeus.

"Oh, please, Dad," begged Laura.

"It can be a celebration for Jack," reasoned Peggy.

"Camping in Ireland…" Thaddeus tried to get a word in edgeways.

"No, not camping, Dad. Staying in a castle. I've never stayed in a real castle before. Oh please, please!" pleaded Jack, leafing through the brochure. "Look at this one – Moon Castle! It's got ghosts and secret passages!"

"Ghosts!" cried Laura. The children crowded round to get a better look at the brochure.

"And it used to belong to a giant," said Mike pointing at the picture.

"A giant?" Charlie piped up above the din. "That sounds like a good story."

"It's miles from anywhere," said Peggy, a little uncertainly.

Charlie took the brochure from Jack and read through the description of Moon Castle. "Looks great, sounds great. Let's go!" she said decisively.

"Sounds creepy to me," said Laura.

"Scaredy cat!" teased Mike.

"There's no need to be frightened, Laura,"

said Charlie kindly. "Your dad'll be there to look after us all."

"Me?" queried Thaddeus. "Why do you need me?"

"It's not that we want your company, or that we like having you around or anything," explained Charlie. "It's just that these castles can be really spooky places and we need a big man around to protect us from harm."

Laura cottoned on immediately. "I won't go without you, Dad," she cried, leaping into his arms.

Thaddeus groaned. He knew when he was beaten.

CHAPTER TWO

Over the water, deep in the heart of the rolling Irish countryside, night had fallen. A full moon shone down on the deserted hills and fields. Along the winding, narrow road, a drunken figure shambled along, singing lushly to the moon. He staggered gratefully towards a road sign and concentrated hard until the letters swam into focus.

"Mooooon Cassstle, to be sure," he hiccuped, turning up the path towards the castle. "To be sure I took the wrong turning out of the pub, and to be sure I've walked for miles." He hiccuped again and swayed forwards.

A sound wafted towards him on the wind. What was it? He stopped. It was a sound like distant thunder, or horses' hooves, getting nearer and nearer. He spun round – and cried out loud in astonishment. The ghostly form of a horse and rider raced towards him across the fields. The helmeted rider wore a dark flowing cloak and brandished a gleaming sword.

The man blinked, unable to believe his eyes, then as the horse and rider came closer, he ran for his life. But the horse was quicker than him.

He stumbled and nearly fell, grabbing at bushes and crying out in panic. Suddenly he fell full length and his cries took on a different, more desperate tone as the earth beneath him sucked him in and pulled him down.

"Help me! For pity's sake, save me!" he cried. The rider reined in his horse but did nothing to help.

"Save me, save me!" cried the drunk again, his arms stretched out to the rider. Still the rider did nothing but watch as the bog pulled the man down. Then he turned abruptly and galloped away in the direction of the castle.

Thaddeus Arnold stepped out of a taxi, thanked the driver and paid his fare. He looked around the busy London street, and at all the people rushing backwards and forwards. A couple passed by, holding hands. Thaddeus winced. What he really needed to do was get out somewhere on his own. He needed wide open spaces. His life was in danger of getting complicated and he needed to think. He walked through the impressive entrance of the Royal Society of Gentlemen Explorers, and was warmly greeted by the doorman.

"Ah, Mr Arnold. Lord Foggo's waiting for

you in the members' bar, sir."

"Thank you, Stanley," said Thaddeus, handing over his coat and umbrella. He set off for the bar, and found Lord Foggo ensconced in his favourite chair by the fireplace.

"So what's the plan, young man?" asked the venerable chairman.

"That unmapped area to the west of the Limpopo, I thought perhaps a quick six months…" Thaddeus started outlining his plans with enthusiasm.

"Hold on, old boy!" muttered the chairman. "Times are hard, Arnold. Expeditions cost a fortune nowadays. Not like in my day." A dreamy look came into his eyes. "A knapsack, compass, packet of Ceylon breakfast tea and bingo! Uncharted wilderness, here I come!"

"Perhaps just three months, Lord Foggo…?"

"I thought that magazine lot funded your expeditions nowadays?" Foggo watched as Stanley shuffled over with a tray of tea. Thaddeus thanked Stanley and concentrated on the hot drink before answering.

"Well, yes," he admitted, "but there are always strings attached. They want me to spend half my time on publicity tours, and giving speeches."

Lord Foggo nodded in sympathy. "And then of course there's that Australian woman you have to put up with, Whatshername."

"Charlotte?" said Thaddeus, smiling in spite of himself.

"Dreadful bother. Must be a pain having her getting in the way, snapping with her cameras and whatnot."

"Oh," Thaddeus studied his teacup. "She's not so bad really."

"Hmm, thought you two didn't get on?" probed the old man.

"Well, we didn't at first," squirmed Thaddeus.

"Ah, getting sweet on her, are you?"

Thaddeus blushed. "Well, I—"

"Pretty filly, I'll give you that. Spirited too."

"Yes, well, she's certainly that…"

Lord Foggo paused for a moment, "Do I hear wedding bells, Arnold?"

"Good grief, no!" Thaddeus's cup rattled in its saucer. "Nothing like *that*, Lord Foggo. But, er, well… the kids adore her. She's taking them to Ireland on her next assignment, as a matter of fact."

"Ireland, eh?" mused Foggo. "There's something you could do for me over there."

"Steady on," said Thaddeus, "I'm not sure I'm going..." But Lord Foggo either hadn't heard him or else was simply ignoring the interruption.

"Our fellow society, The Irish Explorers, are looking for a speaker for their annual dinner, very prestigious event."

"Oh no," Thaddeus shook his head. "Oh no, Lord Foggo—"

"You're just the chap. They'll be delighted."

"But I... but you know I hate giving speeches."

Lord Foggo looked at him meaningfully. "Pity," he said, settling back in his chair with a knowing smile. "We were thinking of funding some small expedition or other between us... joint venture type of thing... for the right kind of chap."

Thaddeus sighed and drained his cup. There was no point in further protest. He'd been stitched up.

CHAPTER THREE

In the gloomy entrance hall of Moon Castle, Mrs O'Moon was dusting a suit of armour. She was a old woman with wiry white hair and a wrinkled face.

"Ma! Ma!"

Mrs O'Moon could hear her son Finbar looking for her but she said nothing, concentrating instead on a stubborn rust mark on the breastplate.

"Ma! There you are!" Fin O'Moon stood in a doorway, almost filling it. He was a tall and powerfully-built young man who might have been frightening but for his weak chin and soft eyes. He was waving something in his hand and looking as angry as he could.

"What this about, Ma?" he shouted.

"Hist your row! Shouting fit to wake the devils," Ma turned back to her dusting.

Fin shoved a brochure under her nose. "And haven't I cause? You scheming old biddy."

"What's this you're showing me?" Ma pushed the brochure aside. "I've no time for reading books."

"Don't play the innocent with me!"

threatened Fin. "What's all this? Advertising our castle for rent?"

Ma coyly fluttered her eyelashes. "Me, is it? Advertising?"

"Well, who else?" queried Fin.

"Sure, 'tis nothing," Ma soothed reassuringly and squirted metal polish on the left gauntlet.

"Nothing?" exclaimed Fin.

Finally Ma turned to her son with a soft smile. "It's for a bit of rent," she wheedled. "That's all. And the company."

"COMPANY!" Fin practically hit the roof.

"Aye, we've seen neither hide nor hair of a person this twelve-month. Not a soul comes here any more. I don't know why."

"And nobody will come here neither," stormed Fin, "not as long as I have breath in my body."

"Ha! Away with you. I've work to do, and so will you soon enough," said Ma, collecting her dusters and polish. The telephone shrilled from the dining room. "That'll be for me!" Ma bustled off to answer the phone, Fin close behind.

"Moon Castle!" Ma trilled brightly into the receiver. Fin scowled and heard the tinny voice on the other end of the line ask a question.

"That's correct!" Ma beamed. Fin glared. Another squawk from the phone.

"An article for a magazine, is it?" Ma went on. "Well, you've come to the right place exactly." Fin tried to cut off the call, but Ma slapped his hand. "Sure, there's stories and legends of Moon Castle that'll make your hair turn whiter than the driven snow," Ma continued as if nothing had happened.

"So that would be just for yourself?" Ma asked in a warm and caring voice. Fin tried to grab the phone from his mother's hand, but she thwacked him around the ear.

"Three adults and four children! Well, to be sure we have room!"

"Ma!" protested Fin.

"And a dog. Splendid! I'll have a real Irish welcome ready for the lot of you!"

Fin turned on his heel and stamped out of the room in a great sulk. Ma finished her phone call and hung up, so pleased with herself that she danced a little jig before setting off in pursuit of her son.

"Fin!" she bellowed, "Fin!" She caught up with him as he trudged miserably through the great hall, nearly knocking over a suit of armour. "Will you stand still while I'm talking to you,

you great obstacle!" Ma grabbed him by the sleeve.

"I'll not do it, Ma!" he protested.

Ma twisted her face round so that it was inches from her son's. "Is it contradicting your own mother now, Fin O'Moon? Aren't they just what we've been waiting for?"

"I'll not take part in any more of your madness, Ma!" Fin tried to turn away.

"You'll do as I say, Fin O'Moon! Remember who you are," she breathed into his face.

Fin broke away from her. "I'm not him! I'm not him!" he wailed. His mother was obsessed with the legend of the original Finbar O'Moon, who had lived over six hundred years ago. She was convinced that Fin was the great man himself, brought back to life.

"You are so," stated Ma, quietly but firmly. "You are if I say so!"

"I'm not, Ma!" quavered Fin.

"You stupid eejit boy!" snarled Ma. "What do you know about anything? Leave the thinking to Ma. She's got the brains."

"I want no more of your madness," mumbled Fin.

"Madness?" she shrieked, dragging her son over to a small door that was practically concealed by a hanging tapestry. "I'll show you madness, young man!" She fumbled along the top of the architrave for a key and unlocked the door.

"Ma!" protested Fin.

"Inside with you! Unless it's another red ear you're wanting!" She shoved him through. Fin, accepting his fate, put up no further protest. "And don't come down till you're talking sense or it'll be no supper for you, Fin O'Moon!" She slammed the door shut behind him and locked it.

CHAPTER FOUR

Thaddeus and Mike scaled the hill behind Peephole that led up to the back road.

"Peggy can be so bossy, sometimes, Dad," he complained. "I'm glad I've got an elder brother too now."

"Well," smiled Thaddeus, "I'm glad your nose hasn't been put out of joint by having Jack in the family."

"Jack's great, Dad. It's not that," said Mike. "But sometimes I wonder what it would be like to do something on my own. Being a twin you kind of get lumped together all the time. You know, as if Mikeanlaura were just one person."

"It's not easy for you, I know," said Thaddeus. "I think you cope very well."

"Well, thanks." Mike squeezed his father's hand. "And it's nice to have you here with us for a change." Thaddeus was away so often on his expeditions that the children didn't see enough of him.

At that moment a grubby yellow van came round the corner of the road they were walking alongside. Thaddeus quickened his pace. "It's Joe!" he said. "Joe and young Tom." He called out to them, and the yellow van chugged to a halt.

"Hi, Mike! Hi, Mr Arnold." Tom's cheeky little face lit up with a grin.

"Just the man I want to see," said Thaddeus, addressing Tom's father. "Got a few broken slates need looking at, Joe."

"Oh, right," said Joe. "I'll pop round when I get back from the horse fair."

"The horse fair!" Mike's face lit up. "When is it? Are you going too, Tom?" he asked.

"First thing tomorrow," said Joe.

"Oh, Dad, can I go?" pleaded Mike.

"Hang on a minute," said Thaddeus. "Yesterday you were begging to go to a haunted Irish castle. I can't keep up with you."

"A haunted Irish castle?" Now it was Tom's face that shone like a beacon. "That sounds great!"

"Please can I go to the horse fair, Dad? Oh, please," begged Mike.

"Let me get this straight, Mike," said Thaddeus. "Are you telling me that you'd rather go to the horse fair than to the castle?"

Mike looked his father straight in the eye. "Yeah," he said.

"Well, it looks like you two ought to do a

swap," remarked Joe.

"Oh, could we, Mr Arnold, please?" begged Tom.

So the following morning Mike bounced off in the yellow van to a gypsy horse fair, clutching his rucksack, his sleeping bag and his independence, while Laura, Peggy, Jack and Tom piled into Thaddeus's car, along with Ruby and Charlie, to catch the car ferry to Ireland.

"The horse fair's OK, I suppose," said Tom, "but when you go every year you've seen it all before. What I haven't seen before is a ghost!"

"Do you believe in ghosts, Tom?" asked Laura.

"I'll tell you when I see one," he replied happily. He was thrilled to be included on the trip.

"Dad," asked Peggy. "Do you think a giant really lived in Moon Castle?"

"It's just an expression, Peggy," replied Thaddeus.

"The Irish like to exaggerate," explained Charlie. "He was probably just some big bully who terrorised everyone into giving him their goods."

"We had a bully at school," added Ruby,

switching off her Walkman for a moment. "Used to nick all the other kids' sweets."

"I bet he didn't steal yours," said Peggy. She knew Ruby very well by now. You didn't mess about with *her*!

"Oh, yes, he did," replied Ruby. "We were all petrified of him. Then one day he made the mistake of trying to nick my little brother's."

"What did you do?" asked Laura, full of curiosity.

"I saw red, didn't I?" she replied. "I got up my courage, marched up to him, slapped him round the face and told him he was a cowardly bully and if he nicked sweets from little kids ever again he'd have me to reckon with."

"And what did he do?"

"Well, that's the surprising thing. He burst into tears and ran off. I don't think he ever nicked another sweet."

"That's right, Ruby," said Thaddeus. "If something really scares you, and you face up to it, it usually does go away."

The children all thought about this for a minute. Then the music-mad, Walkman-loving Ruby said, "I always sing a song if I'm scared."

Peggy laughed. "Just like Mary Poppins!" she said.

"Yeah, well," Ruby grinned. "I bet Mary Poppins didn't know this one!" She began to sing "*Help! I need somebody...*" and everyone joined in except Thaddeus, who was watching the road carefully.

Charlie peered at the map and she and Thaddeus concentrated for a while on the winding lanes and on trying to read unhelpful signposts.

"D'you think they'll give us afternoon tea?" asked Jack. "My stomach's beginning to rumble."

But Ma O'Moon was not to be found in the kitchen making fruit cake for her visitors' tea – she was up in the tower-room laboratory with her son, Fin. Bunsen burners hissed, potions bubbled and a thick green liquid dripped from a distilling jar into a glass beaker. Puss, the castle cat, snoozed contentedly at Fin's feet and Ma peered eagerly over his shoulder.

"Is that right?" she asked as Fin mixed liquid in a jar. "It's not clear like the last time."

"Will you go away, Ma, and give me some peace?" complained Fin. Why couldn't he ever escape from his mother? And why was she so obsessed with their ancestor Finbar O'Moon and his ridiculous potion? He turned away from her so that she couldn't see what he was doing.

But Ma would not be put off. She grabbed at the jar, which slipped from her fingers and broke into smithereens on the stone floor. Puss leapt in the air and knocked over a tray of Petri dishes.

"Ah, see what you've done!" cried Fin. "Now I'll have to start all over again. Out of the way, Puss!" Guiltily, Puss crept away, attempting to clear up the mess by licking at the spilt green liquid. Neither Fin nor Ma noticed.

"Well, it didn't look right, anyhow," said Ma.

Fin tried to be patient with his mother. "Will you go and take your medicine and have a nap? I know what I'm doing," he said in a soothing voice.

"Ah you're a good boy, Fin," she purred. "You're a good boy to your old Ma."

Fin sighed as she shuffled out of the room, delighted that she'd gone. He heard the unfamiliar sound of tyres on gravel and groaned. It was those unwanted visitors of Ma's. Fin walked to the tower window for a better view, taking care not to let himself be seen from down below. He could see the visitors getting out of their car and collecting a whole pile of baggage from the boot. There were a lot of excited, chattering children. His heart sank. How was he going to get rid of them?

"Oh, look!" cried Laura, pointing upwards. Fin quickly turned away from the window, but it wasn't at him that Laura was pointing. It was Puss, standing on the very edge of the crenellated tower and uttering wild, demented shrieks, that had caught her attention. Everyone's gaze followed her pointing finger.

"It's going to jump!" gasped Charlie.

"It'll be killed!" cried Jack.

Prince leapt out of the car and started barking furiously. In the middle of the mayhem, Puss threw herself from the tower, and sailed through the air with an ear-shattering screech. Laura covered her eyes, not daring to look. Puss landed on the grass on all four paws and raced off, howling wildly. The children stared, open-mouthed. How could the cat have survived such a huge jump? And why did it want to jump anyhow?

"Why on earth wasn't it killed?" asked Peggy in amazement.

"I can't think," said Thaddeus. "I had no idea a cat could survive a fall like that."

"Wow!" said Ruby, "I wouldn't want to be a mouse around here. No chance." Everyone looked slightly stunned until Thaddeus clapped his hands for action.

"Bags, everybody," he reminded them. "No shirkers!" Groaning, they turned to help.

CHAPTER FIVE

Laura looked up at the imposing façade of Moon Castle. It held an indefinable air of foreboding.

"It's brilliant," cried Tom. "I want to go up in the tower."

"It's spooky," Laura pronounced.

"It's just old, Laura," comforted Peggy.

"No," replied Laura, trying to pick the right words for what she was feeling. "It's like… the castle's watching us, as if it wants us to go away."

"Well, tough for the castle," smiled Charlie, "because we're here."

As the weary travellers approached the large wooden front door, it swung slowly open with a scary creak.

"Hello!" said Charlie brightly, expecting to see her hostess. But there was no one there. Who had opened the door then? Tom looked behind the door, just to check, but there was nobody there either. Laura shivered.

They entered the gloomy entrance hall with their bags and cases, casting slightly nervous glances around, but it was deserted except for several suits of very old and dusty armour.

Peggy sneezed.

"Hello!" said Charlie again.

"So who opened the door?" asked Laura.

"Perhaps it's automatic," suggested Ruby.

"In a medieval castle? I don't think so," said Peggy, practical as ever.

"It must be the wind, Laura," said Thaddeus reassuringly.

"Hello! Mrs Moon? Is anybody home?" Charlie called out.

But no human voice answered her, just a wild screeching sound. Laura grabbed hold of her father's arm.

"That wasn't the wind," she whimpered.

"Well, what was it, then?" asked Tom. "I wasn't expecting to meet the ghosts quite so soon."

"Sounded like a bird," said Thaddeus, but none of them was convinced. A sudden rattling sound made them turn quickly.

"Look out!" cried out Jack as a suit of armour crashed to the floor from a niche high in the wall, narrowly missing Thaddeus.

"I don't like this place," wailed Laura, once the dust had settled. "I *said* the castle didn't want us."

"Scaredy-cat!" said Tom.

"Maybe this isn't such a good idea after all," said Thaddeus, comforting Laura.

But their fears were soon forgotten as Ma O'Moon bustled into the hall, all smiles and welcomes. She looked reassuringly normal, if a little old to be looking after such a huge place.

"I'm so sorry," Ma beamed, "I was taking a nap…" she caught sight of the suit of armour in pieces on the floor. "Oh my goodness!" she cried in alarm. "Whatever happened? Is anyone hurt?"

"No, we're all right," said Thaddeus. "It just fell from the wall up there," he pointed to the now-empty niche.

"Ah, well," Ma smiled. "What a welcome that must have been for you. I'm sorry. It's caused by the subsidence, of course – the castle's built on an old swamp, you know. Gives a little shake now and then, nothing to worry about."

"Was the castle really built by a giant?" Tom asked the kindly-looking old woman.

"To be sure it was," she replied proudly. "The mighty Finbar O'Moon. My son and I…" she smiled coyly, "…are in direct descent. His blood courses in our veins. Come, I'll show you the man himself. Leave the bags here. My son will fetch them up for you by and by." She beckoned them to follow her into the library.

Bookshelves lined three walls, but on the fourth hung a fearsome portrait that dominated the room. It showed a huge man riding a magnificent-looking horse at full tilt, sword raised above his head. He was wearing a distinctive armour, a flowing cloak and a full-face helmet with just a dark, empty slit left for the eyes.

"My ancestor, Finbar O'Moon," Ma O'Moon announced. She gazed at him in admiration.

"He looks scary," whispered Laura. She wasn't at all happy in the strange room.

"Oh, he was a fearsome man, right enough," said Ma proudly. "A real terror to cross."

"Er… when did he die?" asked Jack.

"Well now," chuckled the old lady. "There's folks say he never did. But that's the drink talking. He's been gone some six or seven hundred years now."

"I'm quite glad about that," Peggy breathed a sigh of relief.

Ma turned and headed for the door. "I'll show you round our castle," she said, motioning to them to follow.

Laura, unable to take her eyes from the

fearsome portrait, lagged behind. Then something happened which she couldn't believe. The slit in the helmet left for Finbar O'Moon's eyes suddenly blazed with a piercing light. Laura blinked, looked again and gasped in horror.

"What's the matter, Laura?" Thaddeus wheeled round and rushed back to her. Laura was still standing in front of the portrait, pointing at the slit in the helmet.

"The eyes," she whispered. "There were eyes looking at me!" She hid her face in her father's jacket.

"It hasn't got any eyes," said Tom helpfully.

"It had, it had," sobbed Laura. "They were looking straight at me!"

Ma O'Moon hurried over with an explanation.

"Ah, you poor deluded thing," she smiled. "Sure, 'tis only the light playing tricks. We've only got the generator for the electricity, you see."

She hustled them out, with a backwards glance at the portrait. Finbar O'Moon looked down upon an empty room. The eyes blazed momentarily in the expressionless slit, and the sound of a low moan reverberated in the still air.

CHAPTER SIX

"And this is the Great Hall," Ma gestured to the tapestry-hung walls. There were also several large and very dark pieces of furniture which gave the place an air of gloom. "The Hall used to be filled with folk, eating and dancing till all hours, but that's all finished now."

"Shame," said Charlie, thinking how bright and lively the room must have looked in days gone by. The children were looking at the tapestries on the walls.

Ma led them on into the next room. "The drawing room is cosier, to my mind. Come through here." Thaddeus and Charlie obediently followed Ma on the guided tour, but the children hung back, waiting for Jack who was wrestling with one of the tapestries.

"There's a door hidden behind here," he said. "I saw the hanging move when we all went past it."

"I wonder if it leads to the tower?" said Tom in excitement. "I bet it does." He peered over Jack's shoulder as he tried the handle.

"Bother! It's locked," Jack exclaimed, pushing and pulling at the door.

"Jack! Jack!" Tom tapped Jack urgently on the shoulder and Jack turned round to find himself looking straight up into the scowling face of Fin O'Moon.

"What are you doing with that door?" he shouted furiously.

"Er…" stammered Peggy, startled by Fin's sudden appearance and his obvious anger. "We're sorry, we thought it led up to the tower, we thought, you know, the view…" her voice trailed off.

"The tower's old and dangerous. Nobody uses it. Now, be off with you!" Fin had made himself quite clear. The children scuttled out of the room, following the sounds of Ma's guided-tour-voice floating from the rooms beyond.

"And this is the last room, the dining room, where we'll be serving you our Irish specialities."

Fin glared and shut the door behind them.

The tour complete, Charlie and Thaddeus found themselves alone in the entrance hall. Ma had gone to find the children.

"I think it's wonderful, Thad," said Charlie. "It'll make a great piece for the magazine, plenty of atmosphere and ancestors."

"Plenty of codswallop and cobwebs," said

Thad, still not happy at being in Ireland at all –
but he said nothing to Ma when she reappeared
with a bunch of subdued children in tow.

"What's the matter with you lot?" inquired
Thaddeus, taking one look at their glum faces.

"It's nothing, Dad," said Peggy.

Fin O'Moon threw open the door on the
other side of the room. "We don't want visitors
here!" he snarled.

Ma in her turn was furious. "Will you
shush!" she said fiercely to her son.

"It's not at all suitable. It's damp and cold.
You'll not be liking it," Fin added quickly before
his mother could shut him up. "It's unhealthy
and there's rats—"

With two strides Ma was standing in front of
Fin. Despite the big difference in size, he was
frightened of her. She had always ruled his life.
"Shut your big stupid mouth, Fin O'Moon!"
she hissed, giving him an ugly, threatening look.

Fin was silenced. Ma turned round to face
her visitors, all sweetness and light once more.
"Take no notice of him. My own dear son, God
help me." She waved her fingers near her head,
and winked. "Not quite right in the head," she
mouthed, wheeling around and glaring at Fin
again. He backed out of the door and Ma

slammed it shut, turning once more to her visitors.

"If ever a mother suffered so..." she smiled by way of explanation. "Now," she beamed, turning to Thaddeus and Charlie. "I've put yourselves in the master bedroom."

"Sorry?" said Thaddeus.

"You and your wife," explained Ma.

Thaddeus gulped. "But we're not married," he replied, looking horrified.

"Are you not?" Ma was shocked.

"No."

"Not yet," Laura whispered to Peggy, and giggled.

"Oh, well, that'll never do then, will it?" said Ma. "I'll get another room ready. Come on, children, I'll show you *your* bedrooms." She swept out, leading the children and Ruby to the staircase.

"Well, you certainly told her what was what," said Charlie, once they were alone.

Thaddeus did his best to ignore her and walked into the library. Charlie followed him. "Stupid woman, fancy thinking we were married," he said, picking up a book and leafing through it.

"Why's that so stupid?" asked Charlie in a

voice full of meaning.

"Well, really," said Thaddeus, holding out the book he'd picked up. "Look, there's some fascinating stuff here." He was desperate to change the subject.

"Is it so unthinkable?" Charlie pursued.

Thaddeus ignored her. "*The Legend of Finbar O'Moon*," he read. "It appears he came up with an elixir of eternal youth. Obviously he didn't hand the formula down to our hostess."

"Don't be horrid," said Charlie, turning round with a bright smile as Ma O'Moon appeared in the doorway.

"Ah, there you are. All ready now," said Ma.

"Thank you," said Thaddeus, putting the book down.

"I'm sorry I took you for being married," Ma apologised. "Only you've got an air of belonging together, you see. You look like a couple."

"Don't worry about it, Mrs O'Moon. It's an easy enough mistake," said Charlie, looking straight at Thaddeus, who shuffled his feet and studied his shoes. She turned back to Ma. "Mrs O'Moon, may I take a photograph of you, against the portrait of your ancestor?"

"A photo?" said Ma fearfully. "Of me?"

"Well, yes," said Charlie, "for my magazine piece."

"Oh no," said Ma, shaking her grey head. "You'll not be wanting a photo of me. I'm old and I'm wrinkled…"

"But—" Charlie protested.

"No one wants to be looking at the horrid old hag I've become."

"Oh, but Mrs O'Moon, you look wonderful," interrupted Thaddeus gallantly.

"Flatterer!" Ma smiled. "Here now," she picked up a faded sepia photograph in a silver frame from the mantelpiece. "Here's a photo of me. How I was."

Charlie took the photo. It showed a stunningly lovely young woman.

"That was just before my wedding," said Ma proudly.

"Beautiful," admired Thaddeus.

"Oh, sure, I was the beauty of the county, right enough. Some said the fairest in all Ireland."

"I can believe it," said Charlie.

"What happened to your husband?" asked Thaddeus.

"He flew out of the door," said Ma bitterly, "when the wrinkles started crawling all over my face."

CHAPTER SEVEN

Laura and Peggy were unpacking in their turret bedroom. As Peggy carefully put Ted on her pillow, Jack and Tom burst in.

"We're unpacked and ready to explore. D'you want to come?" asked Tom.

"OK," said Laura. "Just as long as we don't go anywhere near that picture. There's something about that library that's really spooky."

"Dad said if you face up to what frightens you, it goes away," remembered Jack.

"I don't care," said Laura. "I don't want to see it."

"Laura," said Peggy reasonably. "It's silly to be frightened for a fortnight. Why don't we all go and look at it together?"

Laura looked doubtful, but before she could reply, Ruby poked her head round the door. She put on a threatening voice: "Confess now, and it'll be easier for you. Which one of you nicked my Walkman?"

The children all shook their heads.

"Funny, that," said Ruby, in her normal voice, and she disappeared again.

"Come on, Laura," said Peggy, and took her

younger sister's hand. They all trooped down the stairs to the hall where the suit of armour had nearly crashed on top of them.

"What's the spooky rating on this room, Laura?" asked Jack.

"It's OK in here," she replied. Next stop was the library where the portrait hung. Laura shivered as she walked into the room.

Peggy pointed at Finbar O'Moon. "See, it hasn't got any eyes, has it?"

"Not now," admitted Laura.

"It must have been the light, Laura. A beam of sunlight flashing on the varnish or something."

"Better now?" asked Peggy.

"A bit," answered Laura, "but it still makes me feel peculiar."

"Come *on*," said Tom. He led the way into the Great Hall. The locked door behind the tapestry was as irresistible to the children as a magnet. Jack jiggled the handle again but it was still locked. He knelt down and peered through the keyhole.

"You don't want to be wasting your time in there!" boomed the familiar voice of Ma O'Moon, who had suddenly materialised behind them. "The key's long been lost and anyway the tower's not safe. We never use it."

"Oh, right," said Peggy. "Thanks, Mrs O'Moon."

"Call me Ma," she smiled at them all warmly. "And be off with you now and enjoy yourselves." She stood there with her arms crossed, waiting until they'd left. Then she fumbled above the architrave for the key, opened the door and scuttled up the stairs to the tower laboratory.

Fin, who was hurriedly stowing Charlie's hairbrush into a cupboard along with Ruby's Walkman and Peggy's Ted, looked up guiltily.

"What are you up to now, Ma?" asked Fin.

"You're no son of mine, Fin O'Moon," she said sadly, slumping down on a chair.

"'Course I am," replied Fin.

"You're trying to scare away those folk, when they could be the saving of me."

"Now, Ma, can't you see I'm hard at work here?"

"You know what I want, Fin O'Moon, and I want it now!"

"It's not ready, Ma. I'm doing my best, Ma."

Ma sulked. "What have I done to deserve a son who'd watch his own flesh and blood destroyed when he has the means to prevent it?"

"I'm telling you, Ma, I don't have the means," shouted Fin. "The potion isn't right. I told you about the cat. I've been using the horn of a goat instead of the horn of a unicorn. I can't make Finbar's recipe exactly as he wrote it down – you can't get the ingredients nowadays. And the last lot I made wasn't right. It made the cat jump off the roof of the tower."

"You can get it right, Fin O'Moon. I know you can."

"Ma!" protested Fin, but Mrs O'Moon was on her feet and clutching at his lapels.

"Promise me you'll try again. Promise me! Save me, son," she croaked like a drowning woman, "For pity's sake, save me."

"All right, all right," said Fin, disengaging himself.

"We'll try it on the big one, Mr Arnold. If it works on him, it'll work on anybody."

"If you say so, Ma," sighed Fin, turning back to the drawer where he had hidden Peggy's Ted, Ruby's Walkman and Charlie's hairbrush.

In the girls' bedroom Peggy was going frantic.

"Where's Ted?" she cried.

"I saw you put him on the pillow," said Laura.

"Well, he's not there now," said Peggy grimly.

There was a knock at the door. Peggy snatched it open. The two boys stood outside.

"OK, where is he?" she demanded furiously.

"Where's who?" asked Tom innocently.

"As if you didn't know. Ted."

"Haven't touched him," said Jack, "I swear."

"I bet. Where have you hidden him?"

"We haven't touched him, Peggy, honestly."

"Perhaps it was the ghost who took Ruby's Walkman," suggested Tom.

"Shut up, Tom!" cried Laura.

"If he's in your room…" began Peggy threateningly, going out of the room towards the boys' bedroom, "…you'll be sorry."

"Calm down, you lot," Charlie appeared in the doorway. "It's time you were tucked up in bed. Laura, did you borrow my hairbrush?"

"No, Charlie," said Laura.

"That's odd," she mused. "It was on the dresser, and now it's gone. Ah, well. These things happen. I'm just out for a walk. Goodnight!"

"Goodnight, Charlie," chorused the children, and then they turned to look at each other. First the Walkman, then Ted, now a hairbrush. What *was* going on?

CHAPTER EIGHT

Charlie combed her hair, fixed her lipstick and wandered out into the moonlit night to find Thaddeus. She saw him sitting on a stone bench, gazing at the stars, and walked over towards him.

"Oh! Charlie!" he said, surprised to see her, and making room for her on the bench.

"Sorry, I didn't mean to startle you. What are you doing?"

"Oh, nothing," he replied. "Just thinking."

"About?"

"This place."

"What about it?"

"Well, Ma may be welcoming enough, but her son certainly doesn't want us here."

"He won't be any trouble. Did you see how she shut him up? I bet you wish you could have that effect on the kids!"

Thaddeus grinned.

"Four's quite a handful," she continued.

"Oh, Ruby can cope. She's a genius."

"Yeah, she's great… It's a beautiful night."

"Mmm…"

"Oh, what the heck!" Charlie said suddenly,

as if she'd just decided on something.

"What's up?" Thaddeus looked puzzled.

"I had this all planned," explained Charlie, "Candlelit dinner... soft music... but I guess this is as romantic as anywhere. Thaddeus," she turned to face him. "I think it's about time we got married."

"*Married*?" Thaddeus's voice trembled. He was horrified at the thought.

"Since everyone thinks we're a couple already. It would save on bedrooms."

"But—" started Thaddeus.

"Well?" queried Charlie.

Thaddeus opened and shut his mouth, but nothing came out.

"Thad?" Charlie watched him struggle for words.

He finally spoke. "G-Goodness, is that the time? 'Night!" He jumped up and practically ran into the castle, leaving Charlie to sigh at the moon.

Thaddeus took the stairs up to his bedroom two at a time. He popped his head into the boys' bedroom, but couldn't go into the girls' room because with Prince sleeping across the door it would have been impossible to open the door without firing off a salvo of barks. He tiptoed on past.

Laura tossed and turned in her bed. When the moon rose a couple of hours later, a shaft of moonlight shone on her face through the open curtains, waking her up.

"That's odd," she puzzled. "I'm sure we drew the curtains." She heard the faint sound of a horse whinnying and sat up abruptly. She climbed out of bed and went over to the window. On the dark hillside outside, among the trees, she could just make out the shape of a horse and rider, galloping closer.

"Peggy! Peggy!" cried Laura.

Peggy sat up, instantly awake. "What's the matter?" she mumbled.

"Come here, quick!"

Peggy scrambled out of bed to the window. "What is it?"

"Too late," said Laura. "It's gone now."

"What did you see?"

"I thought I saw someone riding a horse."

"At this time of night?" queried the ever-practical Peggy.

"I'm sure I saw it," insisted Laura.

"It's your imagination, Laura. Like those eyes in the picture. It's this castle. You expect to see things, so you do. Come on, back to bed."

Laura stood there uncertainly.

"Do you want to sleep with me?" asked Peggy kindly.

"Please," said Laura, closing the curtains firmly. "Peggy," she said, climbing into bed with her sister, "You drew the curtains, didn't you, before we went to sleep?"

"Yeah," said Peggy. "So what?"

"Well," Laura yawned. "They were open, that's what woke me up. The moonlight shone on my face." Without further thought, Laura turned over and went to sleep, but Peggy stayed awake for a long time.

Out on the dark hillside, framed against the night sky, a mysterious cloaked rider stopped to rein in his horse. The moonlight glinted on his fearsome, slit-eyed helmet.

CHAPTER NINE

The following morning, the girls were last down to breakfast.

"Did you sleep all right?" asked Ruby, looking at Peggy's wan face.

"Well…" said Peggy, not quite knowing where to begin.

Laura interrupted. She wanted her father to be the first to hear about the mysterious horse and rider. "Where's Dad?" she said, looking around the breakfast table.

"Dunno," said Mike. "He's not in his room."

"Actually, nobody's seen him," said Ruby. "Charlie's had a good look too."

Ma O'Moon bustled in with a tray of tea and toast. "Good morning," she said brightly.

"Mrs O'Moon, have you seen Dad?

"Now, I thought I told you to call me Ma," she beamed. "No, I haven't seen your father this morning. Has he maybe gone for a walk?"

"That's probably it. He's mad on walking," said Ruby. "He's probably made an early start."

"Aye," agreed Ma. "A full Irish breakfast, is it?"

"Oh, yes, please!" chorused the kids, and Ma

O'Moon hurried back to the kitchen.

"Well," said Charlie grimly, pouring the tea, "I do think Thaddeus could have told us where he was going."

"Maybe he's just vanished," said Tom helpfully, "like Peggy's Ted."

"And Ruby's Walkman," Jack helped himself to toast.

"And your hairbrush," added Peggy.

"I expect the ghost got him," said Tom.

"Don't!" cried Laura.

Charlie put a comforting arm round her. "It's all right, Laura, he's only joking."

"It's not a joke any more," said Laura.

"What's the matter, love?" asked Ruby gently, sensing that something was wrong.

"She thought she saw something last night," said Peggy.

"A ghost?" asked Jack.

"Somebody on a horse, outside our window."

Tom draped his napkin over his head. "Oooooh, Finbar O'Moooon!" he warbled in a ghostly voice.

"Tom! Will you stop that! Finbar O'Moon died centuries ago," admonished Charlie.

"Could be the ghost of Finbar O'Moon,"

said Tom reasonably, tucking into the marmalade.

"Don't worry, love," said Ruby to Laura. "It's not ghosts you've got to watch out for, it's little boys with vivid imaginations."

After their hearty Irish breakfast, the children and Charlie set out to hunt for Thaddeus. They looked everywhere in the castle, at least everywhere they were allowed to look, but could find no trace of him.

"He *must* have gone for a walk," said Jack.

"He's been gone hours, Jack," worried Charlie. "Even Thaddeus wouldn't set out on a hiking expedition without telling anyone – or would he? And why hasn't he phoned? I daren't leave the castle in case he does."

"You stay by the phone, we'll look in the grounds," said Jack, leading the children and Prince down the drive. "Don't worry, we'll be back!" he shouted reassuringly to Charlie and Ruby.

"Be careful!" called Charlie after them, and went back inside.

In the dining room, Ma was busy clearing away the breakfast things. She heard her son nearby.

"Fin O'Moon, come here at once!" she

shouted, and Fin obediently scuttled in with a tray.

"You stupid eejit boy," she slapped him round the face with a tea towel. "All I said was let's try the potion on him. There's no need to kidnap the man to do it."

Fin looked puzzled. "But I haven't kidnapped him, Ma! I haven't touched the man."

Ma put her hands on her hips "Then where is he?" she demanded.

"How'm I supposed to know?" said Fin.

"He can't just have vanished into thin air... most inconsiderate of him, just when we need him. Where could he be?"

"You don't think—" began Fin, as an awful thought occurred to him.

"The bog!" cried Ma. "Those kids are out there looking for him now!"

"If you hadn't invited them here in the first place..." grumbled Fin.

Ma chose to ignore his drift. "If he's in the bog, they'll have the police sniffing round in no time."

"And if they drag it, they'll find all manner of things they didn't ought to," worried Fin.

"Well, we better make sure no one makes any phone calls," said Ma. "Be off with you!" Ma snatched up the tray and booted Fin out of the room. "And you'd better make sure that no one falls in that bog," she called out to his retreating back.

Fin skirted round the outside of the house to the Telecom box and snipped the wires going into the house with a pair of sharp kitchen scissors. He draped some ivy over the wires to hide the evidence, and set off at a run towards the peat bog.

"Do this, Fin. Do that, Fin. Do as I say, you eejit boy," he muttered to himself. "One day it's going to have to stop, all this nonsense, all this wanting to look young again, to be sure." He looked around and saw the children safely wandering through the old kitchen gardens, and was about to turn back when he caught sight of Laura, setting off on her own with Prince. They were heading straight for the bog. Fin started to run. Prince stood in front of Laura, realising what lay ahead, barking at her to stop.

"Be quiet, Prince!" she shouted. Prince circled her and barked wildly, but Laura headed on.

"Stop! Stop!" yelled Fin, racing towards her.

Startled, Laura took a step backwards, lost her balance and teetered over the bog. Unable to save herself, she fell headlong into the murky waters of the bog that began to suck her down.

Fin grabbed at her flailing arms but couldn't quite reach. He looked around quickly for something to hold on to, something that would let him reach out further into the bog, but there was nothing! Laura struggled in the deep, dark bog, and her struggles pulled her down little by little. Fin's hand was so close. If only she could reach it. She made a huge effort and flung herself towards him. At the same time he leant over as far as he could, just managing to catch her outstretched hand. He hauled her out of the mud to safety.

"Come on," he said gruffly. "Back home with you. What you need is a nice hot drink." He picked her up in his arms and carried her back to the castle.

Charlie was waiting in the hall, nervously pacing up and down beside the silent phone. She looked at Fin in horror.

"What happened?" she cried.

"She stepped in the peat bog," said Fin, depositing Laura on the sofa, dirt and all.

"Prince tried to warn me," said Laura, her lower lip starting to quiver. She had had a very narrow escape, and reaction was beginning to set in. "I want my dad," she sobbed.

"It's OK, honey, we'll find him," said Charlie, looking helplessly at Ruby. Where *was* Thaddeus?

"Come on," said Ruby, taking Laura's hand. "Let's go and make you some nice hot cocoa."

Fin shuffled his feet. "I'll have to put up a warning sign about that bog. I've seen it swallow a whole cow before now," he said, trying and failing to reassure Charlie. "It's a deadly place if you don't know it's there." Fin shrugged and left her to her thoughts. Charlie swallowed hard, an image of Thaddeus trapped in a muddy grave swimming in front of her eyes.

"She's all right now," said Ruby, returning from the kitchen. "Just a bit shocked."

"Ruby," began Charlie. "What if Thaddeus went for a walk this morning and didn't know the peat bog was there?"

"You mean—? Oh, my goodness!"

"Don't say anything to the children. I don't want to alarm them. I just can't understand why he hasn't rung. If he's not back by lunchtime, maybe we should call the police."

"Oh, Mr Arnold wouldn't go walking in a peat bog! He's an explorer, isn't he? He's been to the most dangerous places in the world."

"Yes," murmured Charlie. "And he generally ends up in trouble..." This was true. Ruby tried to think of something to say that would comfort Charlie – but where could Thaddeus be?

Charlie too was quiet for a moment. Then: "What if the children are thinking the same thing?" she asked.

Ruby headed towards the children's bedrooms from where subdued noises could be heard. "Time to organise a big game of cards!" she said. "Coming?"

"No," said Charlie. "It's just occurred to me he might be trying to ring my mobile. I switched it off to save the battery. I couldn't find an up-to-date power point in this castle to plug in the charger." She raced up the stairs to find her mobile.

CHAPTER TEN

An anguished Thaddeus leant miserably against the door of an isolated phone box quite a few miles from the castle. He had set off for a walk early that morning to clear his head, but it hadn't worked. Uncomfortable notions of love, marriage and commitment were still buzzing around in his brain. He couldn't face Charlie just yet, but he didn't want the children to worry about him. But every time he rang the castle, he got the unobtainable noise. He decided to ring Lord Foggo. He'd understand.

"Ah, Arnold!" said the familiar voice, when he was finally connected.

"Look, I'm not going to be able to make that speech…" Thaddeus began.

"You can't back out now, Arnold," Foggo replied. "It's all arranged."

"I'm sorry, Lord Foggo. I can't— I can't— It's just that at the moment I can't… think straight."

"What about?"

"It's— personal."

"It's the Australian girl, isn't it?"

"No, no, I... er..."

"You can't fool me, Arnold," rumbled Lord Foggo. "We're the same breed. Risk our lives with alligators, poisonous snakes and what have you, but as soon as a gal hoves into view, blue funk."

"I just need to get away for a while, Lord Foggo."

"Quite understand, old boy. Where are you going?"

"I thought," Thaddeus swallowed, "the Ring of Kerry." It was an isolated beauty spot where he had proposed to his first wife. He paused. "I might find the answers there," he added quietly.

"Perfect spot," replied Lord Foggo, understanding the younger man's dilemma.

"May I ask you a favour?" Thaddeus went on.

"Fire away, fire away, old boy."

"I'm going to try to reach Charlie now, on her mobile. But if I don't she may ring you. Please – please don't tell her where I'm going."

"Mum's the word, Arnold. Mum's the word."

"Thank you, Lord Foggo."

Thaddeus put down the phone. He had to call Charlie now. He couldn't get through on the castle number – it was still giving the unobtainable sound. If only he could remember the number of Charlie's mobile! He hadn't got it written down anywhere because he'd left the castle with only the clothes he stood up in, and a credit card for emergencies. What was it? 0468 124 31- 2? or 3? He'd give both a try.

Charlie, Ruby and the children were sitting round the table, staring at their platefuls of food, trying to make conversation. Even Prince wouldn't eat the sausage that Laura offered him. They had spent all the morning in a frantic search for Thaddeus and were terribly worried about him. Suddenly Charlie's mobile rang and they all jumped.

"Hello!" shouted Charlie. "Thaddeus! Where are you?"

"Dad!" cried out Peggy.

Laura hugged Ruby in relief, but it was short-lived.

"Thaddeus, where are you?" Charlie said. "What's happened? – What? – Thad! Thaddeus!" She shook the phone and listened to it again, but it was dead.

"What's wrong?" Ruby asked.

Charlie was stony-faced. "He hung up," she said grimly.

"What did he say?" Peggy asked.

"He just said 'Sorry'," Charlie answered.

"Sorry?" said Jack. "For what? Why?"

"Where was he?" Laura said.

Charlie looked down. "He didn't say," she said. "But it means I've got to find him." She got to her feet and hurried out of the room.

Tom looked at Peggy. "What did he mean? Why did he just say 'Sorry'?"

"It means they've had a row," she said.

Charlie was dialling Lord Foggo's number. If anyone knew where Thaddeus was, it would be him.

"Lord Foggo?" asked Charlie. "It's Charlie Clancy."

"Ah," answered Foggo. "Just put the phone down on your chap."

"Oh, thank God," gasped Charlie. "Did he say where he was? How is he?"

"Gather you two have had a bit of a ding-dong," Foggo said.

"It's all my fault, Lord Foggo. I could kick myself."

"Word of advice, my gal," continued Lord Foggo to Charlie. "We British types are not like your Australian chappies."

"I know," replied Charlie. "You're antelopes, not tigers."

"Exactly. Skittish lot. Worth persevering with, though…"

"I know that," Charlie smiled. "Where is he, Lord Foggo?"

"He told me not to tell you."

Charlie sighed, defeated. "And an Englishman's word is his bond."

"Didn't give my word, my dear," replied the old man. "I'd try the Ring of Kerry if I were you. But tread gently."

Five minutes later, Charlie had swallowed her lunch, grabbed a map, an overnight bag and her car keys and the children were crowded around in the driveway waving her goodbye.

"'Bye! Be good!" she waved back.

"Good luck!" wished Peggy.

"I'll be back as soon as I can," Charlie said to Ruby.

"Don't worry about the kids, Charlie," smiled Ruby. "I'll look after them."

"All this… It's all my fault," said Charlie. "I could kick myself!"

Ruby reached in and touched her arm. "If anyone can sort him out, you can," she reassured her. "You're on an important mission here, and we're all rooting for you. Drive carefully!"

Charlie roared off down the drive, rehearsing in her head all the subtle, sensitive things she was going to say.

CHAPTER ELEVEN

The children trooped back inside, anxious to get on with their holiday.

"Will you come exploring with us, Ruby?" asked Peggy.

"Not me. I'm not the outdoor type. After all that excitement, I'm going to put my wounded foot up and have a cosy doze."

"OK," said Jack. "See you later."

"Keep well away from that bog," warned Ruby.

"We will," they chorused as they clattered out.

Ruby settled herself comfortably in the sitting room. She looked around, imagining what it would have been like when the castle was full of life, and maybe full of music too, judging by the display of traditional Irish musical instruments hanging from the walls. "Ah well," she thought to herself, missing her Walkman, "silence is probably good for you in small doses," and she opened her book.

Ma O'Moon was in the kitchen washing dishes when she heard the children leaving. She stopped what she was doing at once and scurried silently round the castle, looking for Ruby. When she poked her head around the sitting-room door, she smiled at the sight of Ruby resting innocently on the sofa. She hurried to the tower-room laboratory, where Fin was busy studying a reference book. A jar of bright green liquid sat on the bench beside him.

"Is that it? The potion? Is it ready?" she asked greedily.

"I think so. But it's no good now. The man's gone," replied Fin.

"All the better!" smiled Ma. "That's what I came to tell you. We'll try it out on the nanny. Now."

Fin looked uncomfortable. "But—" he started. Ma ignored Fin's feeble protests, grabbed the jar and hurried down the stairs.

Ma looked in on Ruby. She was sleeping. "Perfect!" she thought, and took the potion off to the kitchen to decant it into a homely-looking mug. Ma passed through the library with her precious potion, concentrating on not spilling a drop, so she did not see the eyes flashing angrily at her from the portrait on the wall. A gust of wind wafted through the library and into the sitting room where the nanny dozed.

A loud, musical "twang" woke Ruby up. She

started. Had she heard something, or had she dreamt it? Another musical note reverberated around the room.

DONG!

"Oh yeah," called Ruby, coming to her senses. "I thought you lot had gone out to play!"

TWANG! DONG!

"All right, all right! You've made your point. I'm dead scared, OK, kids? You can stop now. I'm trying to have a nap."

TWANG! TWANG!

Puzzled, Ruby looked round at the musical instruments, but there was no one there. She grinned to herself, got up silently and tiptoed over to one of the huge stone pillars. Suddenly she leapt round to the opposite side, reaching out to catch whoever was hiding there. There was no one. She frowned, then moved on to the next pillar. Same thing. Who was making the strange noises? She nearly jumped out of her skin when the door opened.

"Ah, there you are, Ruby," said Ma sweetly. "Now I suspect you've not been sleeping well, with that poor foot of yours, so I've brought you a little tonic to pick you up."

"Oh, thank you, Mrs O'Moon. What is it?"

"Oh, an old herbal remedy. It's excellent for

reviving the spirits."

"Thank you," said Ruby, taking a sip. "Mmm. It's lovely!"

"Well, you finish that off now. There's plenty more." Ma backed out of the room as Ruby downed the tonic and licked her lips. "Lovely!" she repeated. She looked up at the musical instruments and shrugged.

"She drank it right up," said Ma triumphantly, bursting through the door of Fin's laboratory.

"Ah!" said Fin. "She'll be needing at least one more dose then. I cut down on the strength."

"What!" screeched Ma, raising her fist.

"Because of what happened before, Ma," explained Fin hurriedly.

"Well, give her a proper dose, you eejit! I want to see what happens before that Australian woman gets back with her fancy man!"

CHAPTER TWELVE

The air out on the moorland surrounding the castle was fresh and invigorating. The children rambled along the brow of a low hill, turning back to look at the castle.

"Look, there's our bedroom window!" Peggy pointed out. "You can see your trainers on the window sill, Laura!"

"I was only being considerate to my room-mate," smiled Laura. "They need a bit of an airing."

"Laura," asked Peggy. "Do you think Dad really likes Charlie?"

"Of course he does," she replied. "Why?"

"Because he's got a funny way of showing it," said Peggy.

"Oh, it's only like you at school," Laura explained. Peggy looked blank. "You know – you and Toby Simpson."

"What about him?" asked Peggy defensively.

"You like him," said Laura.

"No, I don't!"

"Yes, you do! You go all red every time you bump into him."

"I do not."

"See, you're just like Dad. Pretending."

"I hope they get married," Jack broke in. "Then I'd have a mum as well as a dad!"

"And we'd have a mum called Charlie!" laughed Laura. But she stopped suddenly, staring at the ground beneath her feet.

"Look!" she said, pointing at hoof marks in the soft earth.

Tom was the expert here. "Horses' hooves," he said. "So what?"

"Think about it. We're on the hill where I saw the rider."

"It wasn't a ghost then. Ghosts don't leave hoof marks, Laura," said Jack.

"Well, who was it then?"

"Finbar O'Moon?" suggested Tom. "Some people say he never died."

"Don't be stupid. He'd be hundreds of years old," said Peggy sensibly.

"Maybe it was someone who wanted Laura to think it was a ghost," suggested Jack.

"The hoof marks are real enough," said Tom. "I should know!"

"And the curtains were opened," said Peggy. "We definitely closed them when we went to bed."

"So whoever it was, wanted you to see

Finbar," said Jack.

"They wanted to scare us," added Tom.

"Or warn us," said Peggy solemnly.

"I wish Dad were here," said Laura.

"It's all right, Laura," said Peggy sensibly. "We've got Ruby."

Ruby was reading in the sitting room when the kids trooped back into the castle.

"There's something funny going on here," said Jack, about to launch into the story of the hoof marks.

"Tell me about it," said Ruby. "I heard you lot, sneaking in here to play those musical instruments."

"What?" said Jack, his eyes as big as saucers.

"Pretending it was ghosts! I know the score."

"But, Ruby, we've been outside, and that's what we—"

"A joke's a joke," interrupted Ruby. "But when you've been found out, it's time to admit the truth."

TWANG!

They all turned round to look at each other.

"That's it!" cried Ruby. "How did you do it just then?"

"We didn't!" they all cried.

Jack put his finger to his lips and crept out of the door and round the corner, but there was no one there. He shut the door carefully, and returned to the others with a shrug.

"Nobody there," he said.

DONG! The note came again.

With one accord, all four children ran to the door and pulled it open. No one was standing there. There was no sound at all.

"Perhaps it's Ma or Fin playing a joke," Tom gulped.

"It's a ghost," panicked Laura. "I can really feel a ghost!"

"Nonsense!" said Ruby. "It's broad daylight."

TAP TAP!

They all jumped, but it was only Ma O'Moon at the door with a tray of drinks.

"Well!" exclaimed Ma. "You all look as if you'd seen a ghost, sure you do!"

"We've heard one," said Jack. "The musical instruments were making a noise, all on their own." Ma flashed a puzzled look at the display of stringed instruments.

"Oh, that happens all the time," she clucked. "'Tis the wind. There's a lot of it about with the subsidence and all. Cracks that the wind blows through. Draughts are the drawback of living history, I always say." She put down the tray of drinks, and handed a mug to Ruby. "Here you are now, Ruby, another drop of tonic for you."

"Oh, thank you," said Ruby gratefully.

"Drink it all up now," said Ma.

"Oh, I will," replied Ruby. "It's great stuff." She drank it down in one go.

"Can we try it?" asked Tom.

"There's lemon barley for you children," said Ma, leaving them to it.

She stormed straight up the tower stairs to the laboratory to thwack Fin soundly round the ear.

"What do you think you're doing, Fin O'Moon, trying to scare them off with your noises!"

"It wasn't me, Ma! It wasn't me!" shouted Fin.

"Don't lie to your mother!" Ma thwacked him again. "You're not to carry on with this. I'll stand for no more of your nonsense."

"I'm telling you the truth, Ma," said Fin. "On my life, it wasn't me."

"So who was it?" asked Ma sternly. "The fairies?"

"Maybe it was the man himself," suggested

Fin in an awed whisper. "Finbar O'Moon."

"You'll be losing your mind, Fin O'Moon," said Ma, but with a little less certainty than before. She put the empty beaker down on the bench. "When will we know if it's working?" she asked.

"I can't say," said Fin. "I need evidence of what's happening to the woman."

"Evidence?"

"Aye, something she's worn today, so I can monitor the skin cells."

"She'll need another dose," said Ma, filling up the empty beaker from a bubbling jug. "This'd better work," she muttered. "All this running up and down the stairs is wearing me out even faster than time."

That evening over supper, the children told Ruby about the ghostly rider and the hoof prints and the curtains, but she remained unimpressed. "There's always a good reason for everything," she said, helping herself to Ma O'Moon's delicious Irish stew. "It's probably all to do with the subsidence. Come on, now. Eat up and we'll have time for a round of Monopoly before bedtime."

Charlie would have given a lot for a comfortable

bed and a friendly game of Monopoly. She'd had a difficult day, driving round and round in circles looking for Thaddeus, until she'd run out of daylight and energy. Sensibly, she decided to get some sleep. She pulled over to the side of the road, and tried to make herself comfortable in the car.

Only two or three miles away, perched on the shore of a lake, Thaddeus surveyed his little camp site, accessible only by a steep, rocky path. A camping shop in Ballymeena had supplied everything he needed, and a man he'd met in a pub had insisted on driving him as near as he could to the remotest possible spot in all Ireland. "No woman on God's earth could find ye here," he'd promised, after hearing Thad's story over a pint of Guinness.

CHAPTER THIRTEEN

Like Charlie, Jack was not having a comfortable night, although it had started off all right. He'd won the game of Monopoly they'd played, and he and Tom had headed off to their bedroom together. But Tom had waited till Jack was fast asleep, and the next thing Jack knew was that there was something – something strange – standing beside his bed.

Heart thumping loudly, he snatched his torch from the bedside table and pointed the beam at the shape. It was a short white figure, floating slightly above the ground and emitting ghostly wails. Jack's lips twitched and he let the torch beam slide down the sheeted figure onto the floor. Underneath the sheet were Tom's feet and the end of his pyjama trousers. With the hand not holding his torch, Jack lifted his pillow off his bed and hurled it at the apparition.

"Ow!" cried out Tom in surprise, and fell over.

Jack leapt out of bed. "Idiot!" he said, and threw his other pillow. Tom recovered swiftly and chucked one back, then used the first one to have a proper fight. Jack, however, was wiser at this game, and promptly ducked, leaving Tom's pillow to fly straight out of the window and onto the ground below.

"Oh no!" groaned Tom. "What are we going to do now?"

Some moments later, with jackets on over their pyjamas and a pair of slippers each, the two were picking their way carefully down the castle corridors towards the front door. Suddenly Jack put his finger to his lips and pulled Tom round a corner. They could hear footsteps coming along the passage. Who could it be at this time of night?

Mrs O'Moon swept past, carrying a small light and a beaker full of green liquid. She didn't see the boys. They gave her a few minutes' grace, then set off again quickly. Jack was worried that they'd have trouble with the heavy bolts on the front door, but someone had obviously been oiling them recently as they slid back quietly and easily.

The boys tiptoed outside into the moonlight, and hurried round the corner to pick up the pillow. As they did so, Jack looked up at the tower, and got the surprise of his life! There was a light on in the top floor window – which meant that someone must be up there! In the tower, where Mrs O'Moon said no one went because it was dangerous! Who was it? Could it be Fin? Or someone else entirely?

"Come on!" he said to Tom. "See that light? That means there's someone up in the tower! Quick! Let's go and try the door behind the tapestry again – I bet it'll be open!"

They hurried back through the front door and to the hall. But to their great disappointment the door to the tower was still locked, and there was no sign of a key. Tom even bent down to look through the keyhole, but there was nothing to be seen. Jack meanwhile pulled a hair from his head and stuck it to both the doorframe and the door itself.

"What on earth are you doing?" Tom asked, puzzled.

Jack explained. "We'll check this door tomorrow. If the hair has gone, it'll mean someone has been through this door to the tower. Then we'll know for sure that there's something strange going on here."

Ruby was tucked up in bed, reading by candlelight, when Ma O'Moon came shuffling by with another mugful of tonic.

"Here you are now," she smiled. "This'll

make you sleep. It's a cure for all ills."

"It's very good," said Ruby, sipping obediently, "Can you buy it anywhere?"

"Oh no," smiled Ma Moon. "It's an old remedy, passed down through the family."

"You ought to put it on the market, you'd make a bomb!"

"Aye, well, there's an idea," a slow smile passed over Ma's wrinkled face. "I'll say goodnight then." And she slipped Ruby's T-shirt under her pinny as she glided through the door as silently as she had entered.

The moon rose high in the sky, and an owl hooted. Up in his laboratory, Fin O'Moon scraped skin cells from the inside of Ruby's T-shirt into a Petri dish. He peered at them through a microscope. At first glance they appeared to be the cells of a 30-year-old woman, but something was happening to them. Fin checked his chart. Some kind of change was definitely taking place.

The next morning at breakfast, Jack spoke earnestly to the others. He told them what he and Tom had seen, and about the hair they had stuck to the door.

"I told you something strange was going on here," said Laura. "First that spooky cat, then the things disappearing and the funny eyes in the portrait, and now this."

"And don't forget the mystery of the curtains," Peggy reminded her.

"Oh, do stop going on about the curtains," said Tom. "Who cares about curtains?"

"Someone opened them while we were sleeping," insisted Peggy.

"So?"

"So how did they do it?" she asked.

"Crept in and opened them, I expect," shrugged Tom.

Laura shuddered.

"Prince sleeps across our door," Peggy reminded them. "No one could have come in by the door—"

Jack signalled to Peggy to shush. Ma O'Moon came in with more toast followed by Ruby, who positively bounced into the room.

"Hiya! Who fancies a run after breakfast?"

The children looked at her in amazement.

"A *run*? You don't even like walking, Ruby," said Laura.

"I can change my mind, can't I? How about you lot showing me the countryside? I've been cooped up in here too long."

"OK," said Peggy, pleased to be getting out

of Moon Castle.

"I don't feel like walking, actually, let alone running," said Jack. "I think I'll stay behind and read for bit." Peggy looked at him quizzically.

"It'll be easier on my own. I'm just going to observe Fin – I suspect he's got a lot to do with all this," he whispered to Peggy as the others were getting ready for their walk. "I won't do anything dangerous, I promise."

And what a walk it was! Ruby galloped on ahead, shouting at them to keep up.

"What's the matter with her?" panted Laura. "She's never like this, and look, she's lost her limp!"

They stood back and watched Ruby bounding through the springy turf. "What's the matter with you lot? You should have loads of energy at your age!"

Peggy collapsed in a crumpled heap. "Whatever's got into her? I've never seen her hurry, let alone run!" she gasped.

"You can't catch me!" cried Ruby, racing off in the direction of the bog.

Ma watched from an upstairs window, a smile spreading over her face from ear to ear.

"Come on! Come on!" cried Ruby. "Who's it now?"

Peggy, Laura and Tom were in a crumpled heap on the ground. Ruby had exhausted them already. They groaned in response to her question.

"We're too tired, Ruby," said Peggy. "We can't play any more."

"Pathetic!" said Ruby. "Just look at me." She rushed off over the field, watched by the puzzled children.

Suddenly, all three gasped in horror. Ruby was heading for the peat bog!

"Ruby! Ruby! Look out!" cried Laura, but Ruby kept on running, not noticing the danger lying in wait for her.

"RUBY! RUBY!" they all shouted together. Ruby didn't seem to hear. She ran straight past the new "Danger" sign put up by Fin after Laura had fallen in, leaping and dancing and waving her arms. Prince barked loudly and the children shouted for the last time. Ruby suddenly noticed where she was – but it was too late. She was going too fast to stop.

CHAPTER FOURTEEN

Laura, Peggy and Tom watched with their mouths open as Ruby took the biggest jump they had ever seen and sailed right over the bog. She landed safely on the other side, quite unconcerned by her enormous leap, and skipped off into the castle.

"Did I really see that?" Peggy asked the others in amazement.

"It must be an Olympic record!" said Tom.

From her window upstairs, Ma O'Moon smiled in delight. The potion was working!

Unaware of the commotion outside, Jack positioned himself behind a suit of armour in the Great Hall, and waited. Sure enough, Fin O'Moon tiptoed across the room, entered the library and shut the door. Jack peeked through the keyhole. He could see Fin take down a big dusty book, then look up at the fearsome portrait of his ancestor.

"I'm not him, Ma! I'm not him!" Fin appeared to be rehearsing an argument with his mother. "It's not right! I shouldn't be doing it. And I won't. I won't. I'll not take part in it any more, you hear? I don't care what you say, it's not right. I'm not him." He shut the book with a bang and stood up, full of resolve. Jack darted back behind the armour, and watched as Fin strode purposefully away down the hall.

Jack slipped into the library and looked at the book Fin had been consulting: *The Legend of Finbar O'Moon*. A soft hissing sound made him look quickly up at the portrait, and what he saw made him back away. A pair of fierce eyes was glaring down at him. The hiss got louder and louder. Jack was too frightened to scream. He didn't know what to do. Suddenly the door burst open and Jack let out a wild yelp. It was Ruby, wild-eyed and bouncing about like a rubber ball.

"Come on, Jack, let's dance! I've worn all the others out. I don't know what's the matter with your generation!" She whirled him round the room a couple of times at breakneck speed and then suddenly flopped, exhausted, into a chair. Jack looked at her, still unable to speak.

Peggy, Laura and Tom crowded into the library.

"Wh-what's happened to *her*?" asked Jack. "She came in here dancing like a dervish, and then just flopped."

"I don't know," said Peggy. "Ruby, are you all right?"

"She's acting crazy," explained Tom. "She leapt right over the bog!"

"She *what*?" Jack's eyes were out on stalks.

"She long-jumped the bog!" repeated Tom.

"And she beat us all at 'tag'!" said Laura.

They looked down at Ruby, who was by now panting and sweating and looking distinctly ill. "Water!" she gasped feebly. "Water!"

Ma and Fin were also discussing Ruby's prowess as a long-jumper.

"Clear over the bog! Are you kidding me?" said Fin in amazement.

"Didn't I see it with my own eyes?" cried Ma. "Her rushing about like a thing possessed. Outstripping those youngsters like she was jet-propelled. It's worked, son, it's worked. And aren't I the luckiest woman in the world having a clever son who can save his old Ma?" She looked around for the bubbling jug. "Where is it?" she snapped.

"Where's what?"

"The potion, you eejit boy! Give me the potion!"

"No, Ma. You know what happened with the others, the side effects. We'll have to wait and see how she goes."

"Give her another dose, Fin O'Moon."

Fin stood up and faced his mother. "No, Ma," he said.

"Are my ears hearing right?" she pushed her face up close to his. "My own flesh and blood refusing to save his old Ma?"

"It's not right! It's all wrong and I shouldn't be doing it," blurted out Fin.

Ma collapsed on a stool and looked up at her son pleadingly.

"Have I lived so long to see my own son turn against me?" she croaked feebly.

"I'm not him, Ma! I'll not take part in it any more, you hear?" Fin's resolve was beginning to wobble in the face of his mother's emotional blackmail.

A tear coursed down Ma's wrinkled cheek. "I'd best say goodbye now. I don't know I've the strength to last another day."

"Ma…" whined Fin

"Yes?" Ma perked up.

"Well, all right. I'll try her with another dose," he conceded.

Ma beamed while Fin poured a measure of potion into the beaker. She grabbed it eagerly and scurried away down the stairs, meeting the children helping an exhausted Ruby to her bedroom.

"Oh, let me help you there," she said kindly. "You look worn out, poor dear." She put her beaker of potion down on the bedside table and plumped up the pillows on Ruby's bed. "Now off you go and let this good woman get some rest," she said to the children. But they stood around, reluctant to leave. "Off with you now!" she shooed them out and came back to Ruby.

"Drink this up now," she offered Ruby the beaker.

"Is that the potion?" asked Ruby.

"Aye, it'll help you sleep. We'll soon have you on your feet again, dancing a jig."

"I've had enough dancing for a while," Ruby sipped the delicious green liquid.

"You get some sleep. Let Ma's potion do the rest."

Ruby closed her eyes, and Ma crept silently from the room, picking up the socks Ruby had just discarded and stuffing them in her pocket.

CHAPTER FIFTEEN

The children met up in the boys' bedroom after lunch for a council of war.

"There's got to be a simple explanation for all this," said Peggy.

"Why?" asked Tom.

"There nearly always is, Dad says," replied Peggy.

"It's ghosts," said Laura, cuddling Prince for comfort.

"There are no such things as ghosts, are there, Jack?" Peggy looked to her brother for reinforcement, but Jack just stared at his shoes and said nothing. "What's the matter, Jack?" she asked.

"I saw the eyes," said Jack in a quiet voice. "The eyes in the portrait. I saw them."

"There! I told you!" triumphed Laura.

"It must have been a trick of the light," said the ever-practical Peggy.

"It wasn't," said Jack shortly.

"Never mind about the eyes," said Peggy. "Where did Ruby get all that manic energy from?" she asked.

"It's weird," said Tom.

"I don't like it," moaned Laura. "I want to go home. I'm scared. Who is the strange horse and rider? How could someone open the curtains in our room without coming in – unless it was a ghost…"

"Or unless they came into the room through a secret passage?" suggested Peggy.

"A secret passage!" breathed Tom. "Why didn't we think of that?"

"It was in the brochure," said Jack.

"So where do we start?" asked Tom.

"The portrait and the eyes," said Peggy. "Both Laura and Jack have seen them, so there must be something that triggers them off. Let's go and find out." The others appeared reluctant to move, so she added, "Has anyone got any better suggestions?"

Jack said, "Let's go and see if anyone has been through that door into the tower – the one where Tom and I left the hair. I bet it's been moved!"

Peggy nodded. "OK," she said. "We'll do that first, and then go into the library."

They all moved towards the door and Prince bounded out of the room ahead of them. They crept gingerly down the stairs and tiptoed into the Great Hall. No one was there.

Cautiously, Jack moved aside the old tapestry that hid the door to the tower. Very gently he ran his fingers over the place where he'd left the hair. It had gone. He turned round to the others.

"It doesn't prove anything," he said. "But I'm sure that someone's been through this door."

"Never mind," said Tom. "Let's go into the library."

And so in they all went. As soon as Prince entered the room, his fur stood on end and he barked like a mad thing. The children tried to shush him up but the best they could do was to sit him in the corner where he growled and whimpered while they looked around. The eye slit in Finbar's helmet was empty.

"Well, now what do we do?" asked Tom.

"The book," said Jack. "Fin was reading a book, that was what made him act weird. Here it is, look," Jack pointed to *The Legend of Finbar O'Moon* which lay on the library table, just where Fin had left it.

"It was when I opened it that I heard the noise and saw the eyes."

"Try it again," said Peggy. "Maybe there's a connection."

"No, Peggy, no!" said Laura suddenly. Prince whimpered painfully.

"Laura, we've got to find some clues, don't you see?" said Peggy. "Go on, Jack."

Jack opened the book gingerly and started to read: "'Finbar O'Moon, a giant of awesome size and strength, ruled the three counties from his fortress, Moon Castle.'" Jack swallowed nervously and looked up at the forbidding portrait. All was quiet, and he resumed his reading: "'He robbed the poor and rich alike and laid waste to the whole countryside…'"

THUD!

A book fell from a high shelf and landed on the floor. Laura howled.

"It's only a book, Laura!" said Peggy. "It must have been sticking out. Go on, Jack."

THUD!

Another book landed on the floor. The children all looked up at the shelves anxiously. Whatever was going on?

THUD! THUD! THUD!

"AAAh!" shrieked Laura.

Books started flying off the shelves, criss-crossing the room like missiles. Suddenly the portrait started to rock from side to side and the whole room seemed to be alive. The children raced screaming from the room with Prince howling at their heels. And they ran straight into the comforting arms of Ma O'Moon.

"Goodness, whatever's the matter? Whatever's the matter?" she comforted them.

"The – the books!" croaked Laura.

"They're flying off the shelves," added Tom.

"And the portrait's shaking!" said Jack.

"That room's alive!" said Peggy.

"Will you listen to yourselves?" said Ma with a broad smile. "You're making no sense at all!"

"It's true," said Tom.

"Everything was flying about!" added Laura.

"Sure, and how many times have I told you about the subsidence?" asked Ma in calm, comforting tones.

"But—" Peggy protested.

"I told you, the whole place is built on a bog, did I not? It moves about a bit sometimes. I've seen it myself many a time."

"You mean, like an earthquake?" asked Jack.

"An earthquake, yes. That's about it. There's nothing to worry about at all. The castle's been settling and shaking for over six hundred years, it's hardly likely to fall down around your ears today, now is it?"

She beamed at the children.

"Oh, you poor things. I bet you thought it was ghosts, didn't you?"

They nodded sheepishly.

"Well, I can see you've had a fright. Come on now, I've made some nice lemonade for you, that'll soon put you right." She put a comforting arm around Laura and led the children off to the kitchen, where she filled them with lemonade, fruit cake and reassurance. Once she'd packed them off outside to explore the cliffs, she climbed up the stairs to the tower laboratory with a very grim look on her face.

"There you are, you scheming young devil!" she shrieked at Fin.

Fin looked up from his microscope. "Look, Ma! It's changed colour."

"Don't change the subject, Fin O'Moon! What do you think you're playing at, trying to scare them youngsters away from here?"

"I don't know what you're—" protested Fin.

"Flying books and moving pictures! You're up to your old tricks again!"

"But I didn't, Ma. It wasn't me."

Ma swung at him. "Don't lie to your old Ma! You promised me to make the potion. And those children aren't leaving until you've finished…" she stopped hitting Fin, and registered the first thing he'd said. "What did you say about the colour?"

"It's the skin flakes from her socks. The cells have changed the colour of the liquid. They're getting younger!"

"So it's working?"

"Well, something's happening right enough."

"So it's right now then, the potion?"

"Well, it could be," admitted Fin. "But I don't know what'll happen to her next."

"Then give her another dose," ordered Ma.

"No, Ma. It's too dangerous. We'll have to wait and see."

Ma scowled her disapproval, but for once remained silent.

CHAPTER SIXTEEN

It had taken Charlie the best part of the day to find Thaddeus. She stood at the top of the rocky path looking down on his campsite. He was cooking a freshly-caught fish over a fire, and seemed very tranquil and contented. Charlie steadied herself with the help of an overhanging branch and continued her descent.

"Is there enough for two?" she asked casually.

Thaddeus spun round, like a man in a trap. He stared at her.

"Hi!" she said.

"But how…?" he wondered.

"Oh, you're not an easy man to find," said Charlie, sitting down opposite him. "I almost broke my neck getting down here to you."

He did not answer.

"You look like you wish I had."

Thaddeus prodded his fish.

"That fish smells delicious. You'd make somebody a great husband, Thad. Oops!" she hit her head with the palm of her hand. "Sorry. My big mouth!"

Thaddeus scowled. He put the fish on a tin

plate and offered her some. They ate in silence. Charlie licked her fingers noisily and Thaddeus scowled.

"Sorry, does that annoy you?" she asked.

"No," he replied frostily. "I'm annoyed that you followed me here."

"You didn't say not to."

"I'd have thought it was obvious I wanted to be on my own."

"Thad," said Charlie gently. "We need to talk. That's why I'm here. I know I rushed you and I'm sorry, but that's the way I am. I'm impulsive. That's what you find attractive in me, I guess." She smiled at him, but he didn't get the joke.

"Attractive!" he bellowed.

"Yeah, and irritating too maybe. But if I was different, we wouldn't be sitting here having this conversation."

"We're not having a conversation," Thad replied. "Do you realise what a smug, arrogant, insufferable, domineering woman you are, Charlotte Clancy?"

"Yeah," she shrugged. "But I've got worse faults than that."

"Well, those are bad enough for starters," said Thad, "and as to the suggestion that I find you attractive—"

"Yes?" twinkled Charlie.

"It's ludicrous. You're not my type at all."

"Wrong," countered Charlie. "I'm assertive…"

"You're a bully."

"I speak my mind…"

"You're rude."

"I'm an oddball, like you…"

"No, Charlie, *I'm* eccentric, *you're* crazy."

Charlie sighed. "How do you want me to behave, Thad?"

"I don't want you to 'behave' at all. I want you to go away."

"Do you want a soft, feminine, fluttery little woman? I can do that, Thaddeus. If I wanted I could use all those feminine wiles and reel you in like a hooked fish."

"Oh yeah?"

"Oh yeah. Make no mistake. You wouldn't stand a chance. But I believe in playing fair. I'm honest. I just come straight out with it and give you a chance to walk away." She looked him straight in the eye. "Go on, then. Walk away."

"I was here first, Charlotte…"

"Call me Charlie," she interrupted.

"*You* walk away."

"Oh no. I'm here to stay."

"Suit yourself, Charlotte. It's only a one-person tent." Thaddeus glanced up at the night sky before he crawled inside his tent and zipped up the flap. Charlie sat watching the opening, unmoving and resolute. And she sat there on the hard ground all night long.

Prince also spent most of the night on the hard ground instead of being on a comfortable bed. He was guarding the door of the girls' bedroom. He'd tried to get into the room but the door was firmly shut – and there were strange sounds coming from inside. What was going on? He whined, knowing he should be in the room, protecting his beloved Laura.

A shadow moved quietly through the bedroom, not waking the girls, but disturbing Prince. The shadow opened the curtains, then touched something high up on the stone wall and climbed silently through the opening that slowly appeared.

Laura, who had been fast asleep until the soft grating of stone against stone had reached her ears, blinked blearily in the moonlight and tried to focus on the shape high up in the wall. She fumbled for her glasses, but by the time she'd got them on there was nothing to see. She heard Prince whine outside the door, and got up to let him in. They snuggled down in bed together happily.

Meanwhile, in the boys' room, the moonlight coming through the open window woke Jack up too. He climbed out of bed to shut the curtains, but as he did so he heard a distant whinnying sound, and the beating of hooves on the ground. He hurried to the window.

"Tom! Tom!" he cried. "Come here! Quick!"

Tom leapt up, not sure what was going on. He came to the window as fast as he could, just in time to see the shadowy figure of a helmeted horseman riding some distance from the castle.

"Finbar O'Moon!" cried Jack in excitement, then jumped as the two girls rushed into their room in dressing gowns.

"Jack! Tom! Can you see him? Can you see him?" whispered Laura, hurrying to the window. She had heard the horseman from her bedroom, and so had Prince.

They all looked out, but the moon had gone behind a cloud. There was silence outside, with not a sign that there had ever been a mysterious horseman.

"He's gone!" said Tom.

"He *was* there," insisted Laura.

"Yeah, I know," said Tom. "We saw him too."

"It must have been the ghost of Finbar O'Moon," said Laura.

"Or somebody who wanted us to think that," put in Jack.

"What?" said Tom.

"Well, the hoofmarks were real, weren't they?" explained Jack. "And somebody opened our curtains while we were asleep. They were closed when we went to bed."

Peggy suddenly realised the same thing. "Ours were too!" she exclaimed. "And they're open now."

"So whoever it was," went on Jack slowly, "wanted us to see Finbar O'Moon…"

"…to scare us!" said Tom.

"But why?" asked Laura.

No one knew. "Perhaps there's something mysterious going on in that tower," suggested Peggy.

"There's certainly something odd about Fin O'Moon. And why doesn't he want us here? Maybe it's him who's trying to frighten us!" said Tom.

The children stood at the window, looking out. They weren't sure what was going on, but they weren't going to be scared away by anybody!

"I'm going to keep watch," said Jack.

Peggy thought she should have her say too. "We'll take it in turns," she said firmly.

"OK," agreed Jack. "You and Laura can sleep in my bed. I'll go first."

CHAPTER SEVENTEEN

The next morning dawned bright and sunny. Ma O'Moon drew back the curtains in Ruby's room, anxious to see if Ruby was still affected by Fin's potion.

"Good morning, and how are you feeling today?" she asked solicitously.

"Wonderful!" chirped Ruby. "I feel like a new woman."

"Ah, that'll be the potion!" smiled Ma. "Here, have another little nip."

Ruby took the beaker eagerly and downed the dose in one.

The children were already in the dining room, wolfing down their poached eggs and crispy bacon.

"So what's the plan for today?" asked Tom.

"Well," said Peggy, "I think we should try and find out why someone's trying to warn us or scare us."

"Maybe the O'Moons have got a secret they don't want us to find out about," said Jack.

"Well," said Peggy, "that awful Fin didn't want us here in the first place, did he?"

"I think he's hiding something," said Jack.

"Well, what?" queried Tom.

"I dunno. But I bet the secret's in that tower."

"But we can't get in there!" Laura said, with something like relief in her voice.

"Not through the door," retorted Jack. "But we haven't found the secret passage yet. I bet it leads to the tower!"

"Maybe someone used a secret passage to get into our room at night," said Laura.

"What for?" asked Tom.

"Well, to open the curtains, of course," said Peggy. "If they hadn't done that, we wouldn't have woken up and seen Finbar O'Moon – which means he's definitely not a ghost."

"I know," said Jack. "Let's ask Ma where the secret passage is."

"She's hardly likely to tell us, is she?" replied Laura.

"She's nice. It's that creepy son of hers who doesn't want us here," Peggy reminded them. "She doesn't want us to leave."

They got up to go and find Ma O'Moon just as Ruby bounded into the room, annoyingly full of beans.

"Who's for a nice brisk morning walk to blow away the cobwebs?" she asked. The children looked at each other blankly.

"We'd rather stay in," said Peggy.

"Wimps! Well, I'm going anyway."

"Someone ought to go with her," Laura whispered to Peggy, "in case she goes crazy like yesterday."

"Yeah, OK," said Peggy. "Wait, Ruby, I'll come with you." And she jumped up from the table, following Ruby out of the room.

Jack whispered urgently to Tom. "You go with Peggy in case she needs help. We'll look for the secret passage."

"Hang on, Ruby!" shouted Tom, scrambling after them. Tom had to race to keep up with Ruby who, by the time he got to the front door, was a speck on the horizon, heading for the cliff walk.

Left alone, Jack and Laura decided to start their search for the secret passage in the girls' bedroom.

"There must be something to press somewhere on the wall," said Jack. He began to run his fingers carefully over it. Laura did the same on another wall, but after twenty minutes' inspection they had drawn a blank.

Fed up, they sat on the bed, with Prince in Laura's lap.

"It *must* be in here," Laura said. "Because

someone opened our curtains and they couldn't have got in through the door. Prince was outside it."

"Perhaps he went away for a bit," said Jack.

"No, he didn't," said Laura. "He never leaves me. He was whining outside the door when I woke up— Hey! The shadow!"

"What?" said Jack.

"Prince woke me up," she remembered, "by whining outside the door. And I saw a shadow, sort of up in the air." She pointed to a corner by the window.

Jack looked at the blank stone wall, and at the curtain rail, which was a long wooden one ending in the same corner Laura was pointing to. He got up on a chair and turned the finial at the end.

The two children gazed in amazement as slowly, slowly, the stone block to one side creaked open. Jack scrambled through the opening, disappearing for a short time, then his head poked back up above the opening.

"Come on, Laura! There're stairs here! We've found it!" he cried.

Prince barked excitedly and leapt through the opening, swiftly followed by Laura. The narrow, winding stairs led to an equally narrow passage. The two children crept along in single file, Laura holding on tightly to Prince's collar.

"We must be in the tower now," whispered Jack.

In front of them a door stood tantalisingly half-open. Jack peered inside.

"Looks like a laboratory," he observed. And indeed it was. Alongside the bell jars and distilling equipment on the dusty bench he spotted the incongruous sight of a crumpled T-shirt and a pair of pink socks.

"They're Ruby's!" exclaimed Laura. She reached over to pick them up and, without noticing, knocked a beaker of green liquid to the floor.

Jack opened a cupboard door. "And look, here's Ruby's Walkman, your Ted, Charlie's hairbrush…"

"Why?" asked Laura, confused. "Who does this place belong to?" While the children puzzled over their findings, Prince quietly lapped up the puddle of delicious green liquid, and licked his lips.

"Whoever it is, there're obviously doing some experiments," said Jack helpfully.

"Fin?" suggested Laura.

Suddenly Prince started barking and howling like a banshee.

"Shush, Prince! Shush!" whispered Laura, but it was no good. Prince spun round like a mad thing and bolted out of the door. Jack and Laura chased after him, along the twisting passage, up and down the stairs.

"Prince! Prince!" shouted Laura, but he had disappeared. Laura rushed on, but Jack stood rooted to the spot.

"Laura!" he croaked, his face frozen with fear, and Laura wheeled round to see what was the matter. Blocking the light on the stairs behind them was the formidable, helmeted figure of Finbar O'Moon. This was no ghost, this was real!

"Run for it!" yelled Jack. He grabbed Laura's hand and they dashed down the stairs, Finbar O'Moon lumbering after them. A little door at the bottom of the staircase looked like the ideal refuge. Jack pulled Laura into the room and slammed the door shut. The children pushed against the door with all their might. Through the grille in the door they could see the faceless helmet of Finbar O'Moon. Laura screamed. There was a dull thud as a bolt rammed home on the outside of the door. Finbar O'Moon turned on his heel and left them, imprisoned in the castle dungeon.

CHAPTER EIGHTEEN

Ruby raced towards the edge of the cliff. "I can fly, just like the seagulls!" she yelled into the wind. "Whee-eee!" And she twirled round and round, her arms spread wide and a manic light in her eyes.

Peggy and Tom puffed up the cliff path. "No, Ruby! No!" shouted Tom. "No, you can't!"

"It's perfectly easy," said Ruby. "You just flap your wings. I don't know why no one's thought of it before."

"You haven't *got* wings, Ruby," reasoned Peggy, approaching her slowly. "Please come back to the castle with us."

"Look! I'm a helicopter!" Ruby whirled out of reach, nearer and nearer to the cliff edge.

Peggy was horrified. "We've got to stop her, Tom!"

"How?" Tom watched Ruby pirouette towards the cliff edge. Then he had a bright idea. He suddenly fell to the ground, howling with pain. Peggy cottoned on immediately, hoping that Ruby's basic instincts were still intact.

"Ruby! Tom's sick!" she cried. "It's an emergency!"

Ruby didn't hear.

Tom writhed a bit more. "Ugh! Aaargh! Owww!" he called.

Ruby paused in mid-whirling.

"What's the matter?" she asked.

"I've got a terrible pain!" groaned Tom.

Ruby came over all sensible. "We'd better get you home, young man," she said, and gathered Tom up in her arms as if he were as light as a kitten. She strode back towards the castle with her burden almost as fast as she had run from it. "Keep up, Peg," she admonished. "I'll give you a piggy-back if you like."

"No – you go on," said Peggy. "I'll be right there!"

But as soon as Ruby was out of sight, Peggy ran off towards the main road.

Charlie's all-night vigil outside Thaddeus's tent ended when he crawled out the following morning and offered her a cup of tea. She accepted it gratefully.

"I'm freezing," she remarked. She had managed to get some sleep, but it hadn't been exactly comfortable, lying on the beach with only her coat to cover her.

"Serves you right for trying to push people

about," was all Thaddeus could think of to say.

"I didn't push you, Thaddeus, I proposed to you." She sipped her tea. "What are you so scared of?"

"I'm not scared."

She paused. "You want this as much as I do."

He poked at the fire. "Rubbish!"

"We're good together, Thaddeus, we make a great team."

Thaddeus said nothing.

"There's nothing to be frightened of," she reasoned.

"I'm not frightened of you!" Thaddeus snapped.

"Well, not of me maybe, but of any kind of commitment. That's what scares you."

"What rubbish!"

"So why do you spend your life travelling round the world avoiding people? Leaving your children alone for months on end?"

"It's my job," Thaddeus answered briskly.

"And why choose such a job? Because you're frightened of getting too close to people. To me. What did you say to your kids? 'Face up to what scares you most', I think it was. Well, it's time you faced up to what scares you most, Thaddeus Arnold: the thought of getting married to me." Charlie finished her speech with a flourish.

"Charlie," said Thaddeus slowly. "I wouldn't marry you if you were the last woman on earth."

"You really, honestly believe that?" she asked.

"Absolutely."

"And that's your last word?"

"Yes. Absolutely."

She looked down at the ground for a moment. "OK. That's it." She got stiffly to her feet and started to walk away.

"Lord Foggo still expects you to make that speech," she said over her shoulder.

"Where are you going?" he sounded alarmed.

"Home," said Charlie.

"To Moon Castle?"

"Home, Thaddeus. To Australia. Goodbye."

"You can't go!" he jumped up.

"Why not?"

"We've got a contract together, for *Scoop* magazine."

"I'll tear it up."

"They'll sue you."

"Let them." She didn't care any more. She

marched purposefully away and started climbing back up the steep path to the road. When she was nearly at the top, Charlie turned back. Out of the corner of her eye she saw him whip around, pretending he hadn't been watching her.

She sighed and resumed her climb, but her concentration had gone and she suddenly lost her footing. Clutching onto the rock face to save herself, the rock came away in her hand, and she was left hanging over a sheer drop, with just one handhold.

"Thad!" she screamed. She hung on like grim death, unable to find a foothold, a small branch clutched in her hand.

Thaddeus, hearing her scream, sprinted up the cliff to a ledge above her, reaching down. "Grab my hand!" he ordered.

"I can't let go! I'll fall!"

"You'll fall if you don't, you stupid woman. Grab my hand!"

Fired by anger at being called stupid by the world's most obstinate, pig-headed male, Charlie lunged herself upwards. Thaddeus grabbed her wrist and managed to pull her up onto the ledge. They collapsed on the road in the safety of each other's arms. When the terror was over, they disentangled themselves and dusted themselves down.

"Um, you'll need a bandage on that arm," Thaddeus pointed to a bad graze. Charlie opened the boot of her car with her good arm, and Thaddeus dashed round to help her get the first aid box. He made her sit in the car as he bandaged her arm expertly. He fiddled with the fastening tape.

"It's all right, I can manage," Charlie grabbed the tape and fixed the bandage herself.

"Like you managed on the cliff, I suppose."

"OK, OK, I'm sorry," she said. "What more can I say? I was stupid. You saved my life. I'm very grateful."

"You surely didn't think I'd leave you up there, did you?"

"Well," said Charlie, "I had just blown you out."

"You'd blown *me* out! Let's get this straight, I blew *you* out."

"OK, OK, have it your way." Charlie was trying to keep her temper.

"So you had to go and pull a stupid, girlish trick like that."

"What? What trick?" Charlie's eyes were blazing.

Thaddeus thought he might just have gone a little too far. He kept silent.

"You think I deliberately put my life in danger, just so you'd come and rescue me?" Charlie's voice was tense with anger. "You think I'd risk my life to get you? Not if you were the last man on earth, brother. Not if you were the last in the universe! Now get out of my car!"

"Charlie…" began Thaddeus, "I—"

"GET OUT OF MY CAR!"

Charlie gave him a hefty push and he landed face down in a puddle.

CHAPTER NINETEEN

Ruby approached the castle doors with Tom slung casually over her shoulder.

"You can put me down," Tom wriggled. "I feel all right now." Ruby ignored him and marched on, kicking the doors open. In the hallway, a frantic Prince leapt up and down, barking fit to bust.

"Hiya, Prince!" said Ruby, finally putting Tom down. Prince was behaving very oddly. He whined and howled and spun himself in a circle.

Tom bent down to soothe the poor dog. Prince yapped in grateful recognition and then dropped, completely lifeless, to the floor. There was no movement, no breathing – nothing. Ruby and Tom looked at each other in horror. Tom, close to tears, cradled the dog's head in his lap, stroking his rough coat.

"What's going on?" Ma bustled through the hall. "I heard all this shouting and barking."

"There's something wrong with Prince," said Ruby. She couldn't bring herself to say the worst.

Mrs O'Moon looked at Tom and Prince. "Oh, the poor thing," her voice was soft and sweet.

"Where are Jack and Laura?" Ruby asked.

"I've not seen them for a while," replied Ma. "And where's young Peggy? I thought she was with you?"

"Search me," said Ruby. "She just took it into her head to run off somewhere."

"Oh, did she now?" said Ma with a look of concern, and she hurried out of the hall.

"Laura and Jack were looking for a secret passage to the tower," said Tom.

"A secret passage? Well, we'd better go and find them," said Ruby. She looked down at the dog. "There's nothing more we can do for Prince. First let's find Laura and Jack, then we'll call a vet."

They looked in the bedrooms, they shouted down all the corridors. They looked in the library, the kitchens, the Great Hall. They looked everywhere, and everywhere they drew a blank.

"There's something funny going on here. I'm going to call the police," said Ruby.

"The phone's not working," Tom reminded her.

"Well, we'll just have to go and find one that is," said Ruby. Just then she heard a faint whimper, then a bark. A rather subdued Prince rounded the corner.

"Prince!" Tom cried with astonishment and relief. "You're *alive*!" Prince barked his agreement. "What was the matter with you?"

"I don't think he's actually going to tell you," said Ruby.

Prince impatiently dragged at Tom's sleeve.

"I think he wants us to follow him," said Tom.

"He's probably in search of supper," sighed Ruby.

"Or maybe he knows where the others are. Come on!"

"Tom," said Ruby gently. "He's a dog, not a detective." But she followed the pair of them anyway.

"I can't believe I've lost three of you," wailed Ruby. "What will your dad say if I lose the lot?"

Prince trotted into the Great Hall and stopped in front of the tapestry that hid the locked door to the tower.

"A locked door. Well, that's very helpful," said Ruby. Prince barked meaningfully.

"They must be up there, in the tower," said Tom.

Ruby rattled the door handle. "Now where would I put the key, if I didn't want anyone to find it?" she mused. She put her right hand up to the architrave and there it was, tucked in a crevice. It was the work of a moment to unlock the door and slip through. Prince bounded ahead and disappeared.

"Prince!" shouted Ruby.

"Shush!" whispered Tom. "We're not supposed to be here!"

In the dungeon, Jack kicked the door again and again and again, not really trying to break it down but because it made him feel better to be doing something. Laura sat on the floor with her hands over her ears.

"Oh, stop it, Jack! Stop it!" she cried. "It's driving me mad."

"We've got to try and get out, Laura."

"Don't be silly," she replied. "You'll never break that down."

"Somebody might hear," he said.

"Who?" asked Laura in disbelief.

"Well, Ruby, or the others, perhaps."

"Huh! Ruby!" said Laura dismissively. "Ruby's going crazy. And the others can't get into the tower."

Jack knew this was true, and couldn't find anything to say that would reassure Laura. He sat down beside her.

"I never wanted to come here in the first place," Laura wailed. "But nobody listened to me, they never do."

"I'm sorry," said Jack.

"I'm scared," replied Laura.

"So'm I. But we'll get out of here somehow."

"Oh yeah," Laura didn't sound as if she believed him. "And what's happening to Ruby?"

"Maybe it's those potions that Ma keeps giving her. But then I thought Ma was nice." Jack thought for a moment. "She seems to want us to stay, doesn't she? Telling us that the mysterious accidents are 'just the subsidence' and all that."

"If she's in on it and the others don't know…" began Laura and then stopped short at a sound she recognised. "What's that?"

"It's Prince!" shouted Jack, scrambling to the door and looking out of the grille to see the welcome sight of Prince barking in the corridor outside.

"Good dog! Good dog!" encouraged Laura.

"Tom! Ruby! Peggy!" shouted Jack.

"Hi, you guys!" said Ruby, through the grille. She unbolted the door and flung it open, throwing out her arms to give both the little captives a big hug.

"Come on!" said Tom. "No time for that sort of thing. Let's get out of here." Prince bounded away and, as they turned to follow, the door slammed shut and the bolt was rammed home.

CHAPTER TWENTY

Peggy was well clear of the castle and heading for the main road. She stumbled breathlessly over the barren moorland towards her objective – an isolated telephone box. She took a moment or two to catch her breath before she lifted the receiver and dialled Charlie's mobile.

Charlie had watched Thaddeus scramble back down to his campsite with a heavy heart. She got in the driver's seat, buckled up, checked the rear-view mirror and was about to start the ignition when her phone rang. "Hello. Charlie Clancy."

"Oh, Charlie, it's Peggy. Is Dad there?"

"Well, not at the minute. What's wrong?"

"I don't know, everything. Ruby's gone crazy. Books are flying off the shelves. Pictures are moving – oh, I don't know. Something awful's happening to us! Please come back! I want my dad!"

"Peggy," said Charlie in her most reassuring tone. "We're on our way. Call the police in the meantime, OK?"

She stowed her phone, leapt out of the car and starting waving frantically. "Thaddeus!" she screamed.

He looked up, scowled and turned his back.

"Thaddeus! Stop sulking, you idiot! The children are in trouble!"

Thaddeus leapt up the cliff path for the second time that morning as if he had firecrackers in his pants.

Peggy dialled 999. "Hello! I want the police—" A large, male hand came from behind and cut off the phone. Peggy whirled round in panic and came face to face with Fin O'Moon.

"I'm sorry," said Fin, putting his hand over her mouth to stop her screams. "But I can't be letting you do that. Me Ma would kill me." He dragged her over to his van and bundled her under a greasy tarpaulin in the back. The ride back to the castle was bumpy, dark and uncomfortable.

Fin helped her out of the van and marched her to the locked tower door.

"Wh-what are you going to do?" Peggy whimpered.

"You'll be joining your friends," said Fin, pushing her along the narrow passage to the bolted door of the dungeon.

Ma appeared round the corner.

"Well, isn't that a pretty sight?" she beamed, opening the door and thrusting Peggy in with the others. "One big happy family."

"Peggy!" exclaimed Ruby. "Well, at least I've found you all."

"Let us out of here!" yelled Jack.

"Oh, I will soon enough," said Ma from the other side of the grille. "Don't fret."

"Let us out now! What are you playing at, you old witch?"

"Oh, it's not playing, my dear." She pressed her wrinkled face against the grille. "It's a matter of life and death."

"You're mad!" cried Ruby. "Let us out of here!"

"Patience, patience," cooed Ma. "And you'll come to no harm." Her long skirts rustled as she walked away.

"Now what?" asked Laura. "There's no one to help us now."

"Where's Prince?" said Tom.

"He must have run off," replied Peggy.

"He'll get help," said Laura positively.

"Oh yeah?" said Jack. "He talks as well, does he?"

A loud thump made them turn round before Laura could think of a suitable reply to this.

Ruby had flopped to the floor like a lifeless doll.

"I'm worn out," she croaked. "I could do with some of that potion."

"No, Ruby," cried Laura. "That's the stuff that makes you go crazy."

"Crazy? Me? What cheek…" Ruby dropped suddenly into a deep sleep. The children gasped, thinking the worst.

Peggy checked her breathing. "It's OK," she said. "She's just fallen asleep."

"Great timing," murmured Jack.

Ruby muttered and mumbled incoherently in her sleep.

"Poor Ruby," said Laura, stroking her hand. "What have they done to her?"

"We've got to get help," said Tom.

"It's no use, Tom," answered Jack. "We can't get out of here."

Up in the tower-room laboratory Fin wiped up the contents of the spilt beaker.

"Can you make some more?" asked Ma urgently.

"Well, I could," said Fin reluctantly.

"What are you waiting for?" barked Ma. "We've got to finish the experiment. It's never gone so well before. We're nearly there, aren't we?" Her tone softened. "Aren't we nearly there, Fin O'Moon?"

"Aye, I suppose," he replied. "But what if Mr Arnold goes to the police?"

"Leave that lot to me," answered Ma.

"We don't want to harm them," said Fin. "I just wish they'd never come."

"We'll let them go the minute you finish the potion for me. I'll not care about anything then." She squeezed his hand. "You're a good son to your old Ma, Fin O'Moon. The best son a mother ever had." She shot him a smile over her shoulder and closed the door quietly behind her, leaving him to his bubbling jars and beakers.

Fin sighed deeply. He went over to a locked cupboard and took out the old manuscript on which was written Finbar O'Moon's formula for the Elixir of Life. He spread it out on his laboratory bench and checked through the ingredients. The jar in his hand started to vibrate as if it had a life of its own. Fin stared at it in amazement. The very floor under his feet started to shake, the bottles and jars on the shelves rattled and broke. Fin dropped the jar he was holding and the whole room started to move as if a giant had picked it up and shaken it. A low moaning sound filled his ears.

"NO, NO!" it groaned.

Jars and bottles exploded around Fin as he fled from the tower room and raced down the stairs as if chased by demons. He staggered into the library and addressed himself to the portrait of his fearsome ancestor.

"Leave us alone. Please just leave us alone. Can you not rest in peace, man? Have you not done enough harm already?"

The door flew open and Ma entered, her face like thunder.

"What in heaven's name do you think you're at?" she cried.

"Nothing," replied Fin guiltily. "I keep telling you it's not me, Ma."

"Nothing, is it? I've just come down from your laboratory, Fin O'Moon. It's nothing to destroy a life's work, is that what you're saying? It's nothing to smash up all your little jars and whatnot like you were trying to break your mother's heart! It's nothing, all this shaking and moaning, driving people away when we need them?"

"Sure I did my best to scare them away, Ma," said Fin, trying to explain. "I did pretend I was Finbar, I pinched their bits and pieces, yes. But as to the rest," he spoke very clearly and slowly,

"IT WASN'T ME!"

Ma sniffed in disbelief. "There's no ghosts here. It's just the subsidence."

Fin was desperate. "Can't you realise it's Finbar himself telling us to stop? It's madness to go on!"

"Is it madness to be on the very brink of a wonderful new potion which will bring joy to millions and make us as rich as Midas himself?" queried Ma.

"The whole thing is madness," Fin slumped down in a chair. "We can't go forwards and we can't go back. We can't let the prisoners go. We can't let their father and Whatshername get back here and find out what's happened, you know we can't. If they tell the police, they'll find out about the others, those poor creatures who went mad after they drank the potion."

"That was nothing to do with us!" protested Ma. "Just because people take it into their heads they can fly, and throw themselves off the top of our tower, it's nothing to do with us!"

"We gave them the potion, Ma. Of course it was!"

"It was for the benefit of mankind," beamed Ma. "It's the Elixir of Life. It'll make folks young again and live for ever, like the great

Finbar O'Moon himself!" Fin looked unconvinced. "When was any great breakthrough made without a few little sacrifices along the way?"

Ma gazed intently at the portrait and then went on: "When we have this potion, the world will forgive us everything. We will be the ones with the power, and those who want it will protect us."

She took his arm gently. "Come on now, son. We're nearly there. Can't you just see your old Ma, young and beautiful again like she used to be? The fairest in the whole wide land… Come on now, son. For your Ma. For your old Ma."

Almost mesmerised, Fin allowed himself to be led back to the laboratory.

CHAPTER TWENTY-ONE

Thaddeus handled the car like a man possessed. They were nearly at the castle, but it had been a hair-raising drive.

"Slow down, Thad!" pleaded Charlie.

"I've got to get to the children, Charlie. I should never have left them!" He took a bend at alarming speed.

Charlie braced herself and tried to talk calmly. "Peggy was going to call the police. I'm sure they'll be all right."

"Fine, but they're still my kids." The tyres squealed in protest.

"I'm sure they'd rather you arrived in one piece, Thad," Charlie gritted her teeth. "Oh, no! What's that?" she screamed.

Something was hurtling towards them in the middle of the road. Thad swerved violently. With more squealing of tyres and a loud thump, the car skidded off the road and ended up in the ditch.

Thad and Charlie sat shocked but unhurt in silence.

"Are you all right?" whispered Thaddeus.

"Yes…" she replied.

"Sorry!" he swallowed hard.

"Forget it," said Charlie. "What was it in the road?" The answer came wagging and barking to the window.

"Prince!" they shouted in unison.

"What's he doing out here?" asked Thad.

"Coming for help maybe," suggested Charlie. "I think we'd better hurry."

Thad scrambled out of the car to inspect the damage. "We'll have to go on foot, the front axle's a write-off." He helped Charlie from the passenger seat and Prince leapt ahead of them, barking urgently.

"Let's get a move on," said Thad, setting off at a sprint.

In his wrecked laboratory, Fin had managed to make up another jarful of potion under the watchful eye of his mother. He held the jar up to the light and nodded, satisfied.

"Is that it now?" asked Ma eagerly.

"Aye," replied Fin. Ma poured herself a beaker of the strange green liquid and held it to her lips.

"You shouldn't do this, Ma," begged Fin. "What about the side effects?"

Ma paused and smiled. "Tell you what, just

to be on the safe side, one last little test." She hurried down the stairs and stopped outside the dungeon door.

"I've brought a little something for your nanny," she said to the children through the grille. "Is she awake now?"

"No!" spat Jack.

"You monster!" cried Laura.

Ma smiled her most charming smile and pushed the beaker through the grille.

"Wake her up now, and let her take a drop," ordered Ma.

"No way!" they cried.

There was a roar behind them. Ruby leapt up, full of life once more, and charged forwards.

"Gangway!" she shouted and hurled herself at the door, scattering the kids in her wake. Ma snatched back the beaker of precious liquid and darted off.

Ruby ran back to the far wall and launched herself at the door again with superhuman strength. With a rending of metal, the bolt fixing flew off and the door swung open. The kids stood there, stunned.

"What are we waiting for?" roared Ruby. "Christmas?" She plunged ahead of them in hot pursuit of Ma. But when she reached the staircase, instead of thundering down it, she headed up, up, up. "I can fly!" she cried, "I can fly!"

"No, you can't, Ruby!" Laura shouted after her, "No, you can't!" Ruby shot up the tower steps with Laura chasing at her heels.

Charlie and Thaddeus raced towards Moon Castle as if their lives depended on it.

"I'm out of breath!" panted Charlie. Prince bounded onwards and Thaddeus urged himself on, even though his lungs were bursting. The shadow of Moon Castle was etched on the horizon and lights flickered in the windows.

Suddenly they heard a whinnying sound and the thrum of horses' hooves on the night air, getting closer all the time. With horror they saw the ghostly figure of Finbar O'Moon racing towards them across the moorland. Thaddeus and Charlie instinctively changed direction, stumbling onwards towards the castle and the children who needed them. In the darkness the "Danger" sign marking the peat bog was as good as invisible.

"Thad! Stop!" yelled Charlie, when she finally saw it, but it was too late. They plunged into the swampy bog, watched from the shadows by the towering, helmeted figure of Finbar O'Moon.

Charlie struggled for a foothold and sunk immediately as far as her waist.

"Don't struggle," said Thaddeus, trying to remain calm. "It only makes you sink faster."

"I'm sorry," Charlie bit back her tears. "I'm sorry."

"What for?" asked Thaddeus. They were stuck fast, facing each other but just out of reach and sinking slowly.

"It's all my fault. I insisted on coming here. Me and my pig-headedness."

"It's not your fault. I ran off. I left the children."

"That was my fault too. Forgive me."

"There's nothing to forgive. You were right all along. I ran away from what scared me most. Commitment. But I won't now. I love you, Charlie, and I want to marry you."

He stretched out his hand as far as he could, Charlie reached towards him and their fingertips just touched.

"You've got a lousy sense of timing, Thad," said Charlie dryly.

A low moan filled the air. The peat bog shivered, and a ghostly voice spoke from thin air.

"PIETRA O'MOON…" the voice sounded across the centuries. Inside Moon Castle, Ma lifted the brimming beaker to her lips. "NO MORE…" came a voice from beyond the grave and the beaker fell from her trembling fingers and broke into a thousand pieces on the stone-flagged floor.

"FIN O'MOON," the voice thundered from the air itself. "IT MUST END HERE. IT MUST END NOW!"

The horseman jolted out from the shadows and lifted the visor of his sinister helmet. It was Fin.

"I hear you, Finbar," he cried. "There'll be no more of it. You can rest in peace now!"

Fin quickly unfurled a rope from his saddle and threw it so that it landed between the sinking pair. It was tied at one end to the pommel of his saddle. Thaddeus grabbed the other end with one hand and with a huge effort lunged across to Charlie so that he could clasp her coat sleeve firmly. The horse, urged on by Fin, began to walk slowly away from the bog, gradually dragging the two adults from the mire. When they were free of the mud, Fin reeled in the rope and turned the horse's head towards the castle. Thaddeus stood up first and hugged

Charlie in relief. After a few minutes, Charlie disentangled herself.

"So now that we're both going to live to a ripe old age," she said lightly, wiping the mud from her hands on a piece of grass, "does the offer still stand?"

"You betcha!" smiled Thad. "But we haven't got time to stand around and get romantic. Get a move on, woman!" He grabbed her arm and ran towards the castle.

They arrived, breathless, in the drive where Jack, Peggy and Tom stood looking up at the tower in horror. Ruby, astride the edge of the tower roof, arms spread wide, was singing at the top of her voice.

"*It's just an illusion,*" she sang, "*that's cheating my heart. It's just an illusion...*"

"Oh, Dad!" cried Peggy, throwing her arms round Thaddeus, regardless of the black mud on his clothes. "She's gone crazy! She's going to jump!"

"Laura's up there with her," explained Jack urgently, "but there's no way she can hold Ruby back!"

Ruby whirled her arms, in preparation for the launch. Laura took a bold step forwards. "Ruby, you can't fly," she called. "Please come down."

"*It's just an illusion...*" sang Ruby.

"Yes, that's it, Ruby," said Laura, joining in the song. "*It's just an illusion...*"

Ruby turned. "*It's just an illusion...*" her voice trailed off as she recognised Laura through the fog in her head. Ruby looked down, suddenly realising the danger she was in.

"HELP!" she screamed, reaching out to Laura.

Thaddeus, Charlie and the others followed Fin to the library where Ma lay prone on the floor.

"Ma!" cried Fin, dashing over to her. "You didn't drink the potion, did you?" he said with concern.

Ma raised her head and looked about her, completely dazed.

"Finbar spoke to me!" she whispered. "He spoke to me. He said we can never use the potion, he told me—"

"I know, Ma," Fin said gently. "It's all over now." He took an ancient scroll from inside his armour. "We'll end it now," he said, throwing the parchment into the fire. "And then we'll call the police. We'll tell them everything."

The flames licked at the ancient manuscript,

the castle shook a little and, as the flames burned brighter, reducing the formula for the Elixir of Life to ashes, Finbar O'Moon's restless spirit gave one last moan and sank to its rest.

CHAPTER TWENTY-TWO

Joe's old yellow van ground to a halt outside Peephole and Mike leapt out to greet his father.

"Did you have a good time, Mike?" asked Thaddeus.

"Brilliant!" smiled Mike. "The best ever. I got to ride a horse, and everything."

"Just wait till we tell you what happened to us," said Laura, giving her twin brother a big hug.

"Come on inside," said Charlie. "I think Ruby's put the kettle on."

As they approached the house, they heard the phone ringing.

"Oh no!" wailed Laura. "That'll be another expedition for Dad. We've only just got back and he'll be going away again."

They could hear Thaddeus's voice as he answered the phone.

"Ah, yes, Lord Foggo, we're back safe and sound."

"Splendid speech you gave last night. Inspired!" Lord Foggo's voice boomed down the phone.

"Well, that's thanks to Charlotte. She made

me do it," answered Thaddeus.

"Oh, taking orders from gals now, eh? Is this going to be a habit?" joked the old man.

"I guess so, Lord Foggo," replied Thaddeus. "It'll be a lot easier for her to issue orders once she's my wife," he smiled at Charlie.

The kids went wild.

"Brilliant!"

"Terrific!"

"About time too!" they all shouted at once.

"I guess that's a 'yes' then?" Charlie beamed, gathering all the children in her arms for a hug.

"This calls for a special treat," Ruby called from the kitchen, and she emerged with a cake.

"That's lovely," said Charlie, smiling at Ruby. The children stared at the cake, backing off a little as if Ruby had presented them with a bomb.

"Now that you're joining the family too," Jack whispered to Charlie, "there's something you should know…"

"Don't worry!" Ruby said with a grin. "I didn't bake it myself."

"Ruby's cakes are more lethal than Fin's potion," said Jack. "You have been warned."

Order Form

To order direct from the publishers, just make a list of the titles you want and fill in the form below:

Name

....

Address

....

....

....

Send to: Dept 6, HarperCollins Publishers Ltd, Westerhill Road, Bishopbriggs, Glasgow G64 2QT.

Please enclose a cheque or postal order to the value of the cover price, plus:

UK & BFPO: Add £1.00 for the first book, and 25p per copy for each additional book ordered.

Overseas and Eire: Add £2.95 service charge. Books will be sent by surface mail but quotes for airmail despatch will be given on request.

A 24-hour telephone ordering service is available to holders of Visa, MasterCard, Amex or Switch cards on 0141-772 2281.

Collins
An *Imprint of* HarperCollins*Publishers*